HILARY MCKAY

FOREVER ROSE

MACMILLAN CHILDREN'S BOOKS

First published in Great Britain in 2007 by Hodder and Stoughton

This updated edition published 2021 by Macmillan Children's Books
an imprint of Pan Macmillan
The Smithson, 6 Briset Street, London EC1M 5NR
EU representative: Macmillan Publishers Ireland Limited,
Mallard Lodge, Lansdowne Village, Dublin 4
Associated companies throughout the world
www.panmacmillan.com

ISBN 978-1-5290-3327-4

1 3 5 7 9 8 6 4 2

A CIP catalogue record for this book is available from the British Library.

Printed and bound by CPI Group (UK) Ltd, Croydon CR0 4YY

MIX
Paper from
responsible sources
FSC® C116313

For Sara Gatland, a very special reader.
We have fixed the date for you at last!
Love from Hilary McKay
(Wednesday 13th December)

Exactly the Sort of Thing I Call Magic

I do not like it when people shout.

Particularly when the person shouting is Mr Spencer.

(Mr Spencer, the new and irritated teacher of Class 6.)

I especially do not like it when Mr Spencer is shouting at me.

School is no longer a peaceful place where you can catch up on your daydreaming, forget your family (or what is left of your family) and talk about things like *Doctor Who* and how to stop Climate Change (we all know how but we don't stop it) and if it is OK for boys to wear pink and all those other things we talk about.

School, says Mr Spencer, is an educational establishment.

And education is learning facts to write down in tests.

Called SATs.

These new ideas do not stay in my head very well, they drift away and before I know it I am back in the good-old-days ways, staring out of the window.

Hence (good word which will get me no marks if I

continue to spell it the same way as the name of those birds which lay eggs – hopefully free range – says Mr Spencer).

Hence the big shouts from Mr S.

At me, Rose Casson, aged eleven, perfectly warm and sleepy by the radiator, watching the rain and counting the sodden leaves left on the sycamore tree in the playground. Twenty-seven at lunchtime. Eighteen now.

I was sitting with my best friend Kiran. I am so lucky to have Kiran for a best friend. Not only because she is kind and funny and pretty, but also because she is very intelligent and does my worksheets for me whenever possible so I get good marks and am not put down into Bottom Set. Bottom Set (who were politely called Gold Team until very recently) are all either football nutters or saving-up-for-pony girls. I wouldn't fit in there very well at all. Except maybe with Kai. He is a Bottom Set football nutter, but has a subsidiary interest in Practical Jokes.

Mr Spencer's voice made me jump, it was so sudden and so hard.

'Rose Casson! I am warning you!' he snapped.

'What, me?' I asked, amazed. 'Why me? Warning me about what?'

But Mr Spencer, who had swung round from the board to shout at me, turned his back in a very deliberate way and carried on writing.

'I wasn't doing anything!' I protested to his back because we've had to learn to put up with Mr Spencer's bad manners here in Class 6.

So Mr Spencer twisted around very slowly and gave me one of his dead-eyed looks and said, 'I will not tell you another time!'

'I don't know what you've told me *this* time,' I said, rather scared now, but sticking up for myself. 'Or what you are warning me about because I wasn't—'

'Rose Casson!' interrupted Mr Spencer in a voice that shook the windows. 'Your behaviour in class is idleness personified! Your standard of work is consistently appalling! And *how many times do you have to be told to stop staring out of that window?*'

I dropped my head and grabbed a pencil and began to draw very fast on my jotter cover. Being shouted at makes me feel terrible. I wanted to push Mr Spencer out the window. Or run away. Or both. Shouting also makes my hands shake. They shook so much I dropped my pencil and it rolled on to the floor.

Kiran shoved me with her elbow and hissed, 'Stop it, Rose! Don't be useless! Smile at him!'

As if to encourage me she smiled at him herself,

angelically (although showing all her teeth). He gave her a suspicious look but turned back to the board.

Kiran squeezed my hand and Molly picked up my pencil and after that I was all right again.

Molly is a girl who tags along with Kiran and me. She is a bit younger than us (ten) and she is a Brownie. We don't really mind her tagging on. She's very nice.

But.

(((((((Boring.)))))))

I would never say that out loud to anyone.

Kiran isn't boring; she is brilliant. And she's Mr Spencer's enemy. She fights him and she wins. She fought him at Circle Time this afternoon to pay him back for shouting at me.

Circle Time is how Mr Spencer fills in the end of the day when he can't be bothered to try and teach us any longer. We have to sit in a circle and take turns to talk about whatever subject Mr Spencer chooses. Of course, you don't have to say anything when it comes to your turn. You can say 'Pass' instead.

But saying 'Pass' isn't an easy option. It causes Mr Spencer to snigger.

So, Circle Time. Everyone taking as long as possible to

arrange the chairs and settle down, and dozens of glances at the clock to see how long it is until home time. Thirty-eight minutes. *Still* thirty-eight minutes! I was sure it was thirty-eight minutes the last time I looked.

The clock must be broken.

Then Mr Spencer announced the Circle Time subject for that day.

'The Worst Thing I Have Ever Done,' he said. 'That should be interesting!'

He put his hands behind his head and leaned back in his chair with his pale moustache spread hairily into the shape of a smile.

On the wall in front of me the clock was still refusing to admit that it was less than thirty-eight minutes till home time. All around people were very quiet, each of us hurrying to stow our private memories into the most secret corners of our minds. Behind me, I heard Kai swallow.

Poor Kai. He knows now that dialling 999 and calling out the police, ambulance, and fire brigade to his mother's fortieth birthday party was completely unfunny and ruined the whole evening. He's only just finished writing the letters of apology.

And they cancelled his birthday party.

At the moment it isn't kind to remind Kai of anything to do with parties, or mothers, or the emergency services.

But Mr Spencer isn't kind.

Mr Spencer must have heard the rumours.

'*Whom* shall we pick to start?' he asked, his moustache stretched even wider. 'Kai?'

'Pass,' said Kai and began struggling with the knots in his shoelaces.

'Pass?' repeated Mr Spencer, his voice high with delight. 'Well, well! Obviously the memories are still too painful! Molly, then? Oh dear. Clearly not.'

Molly had hidden her face in her hands.

'Kiran?'

At first Kiran looked like she had not heard her name.

'Kiran?' said Mr Spencer. 'Hmmm?'

Time stopped. The clock, which was obviously on Mr Spencer's side, refused to concede a minute. Molly's face remained hidden. Kai's shoelaces still would not loosen. Mr Spencer looked as pleased with himself as ever.

It was as if the whole world waited to hear what Kiran would say.

Kiran flicked back her plaits, a battle gesture that should have frightened Mr Spencer, but didn't.

'Kiran?' he repeated.

'I think,' said Kiran softly, looking straight at Mr Spencer, 'we should choose you.'

Oh, wonderful Kiran! Because Mr Spencer went red and then redder, and his hairy smile vanished and was replaced by something that looked like a dead caterpillar draped over a slit, and we saw that he too had memories in the secret corners of his mind that he preferred to keep private.

So we had silent reading until the bell went, and it rang almost as soon as we had got our books out to begin.

Even though the broken clock still said thirty-eight minutes till home time.

And that is exactly the sort of thing I call magic.

Molly and I left school together. I was feeling very good because of the magic broken clock, but Molly was unhappy. Poor old Mollipop. But why did she run after me to tell me she was miserable, and then refuse to say why?

'Stop asking!' she snapped, like I really annoyed her.

Hmmm.

I probably do annoy Molly because I'm not like her in any way and I don't know why she bothers with me.

It may be because of Caddy.

Caddy, my big sister aged twenty-three, who is kind, daft and hasn't been seen for ages. (In fact it is just like she has totally vanished from the face of the earth except for a few crackly phone calls and some animated e-mails that don't always load.)

But (a word you're not supposed to use to begin sentences and which will cause Mr Spencer to draw big red aggravated rings around it pressing so hard with his pencil that it goes through to the next page) Molly admires Caddy very, very much. They are both fascinated by Natural History of the exotic David Attenborough variety. Molly used to come round to our house just to look at Caddy, and when Caddy got herself a job in the nearby zoo Molly was so impressed she begged me to ask for her autograph.

So I did and Caddy wrote on the back of a Zoo Map postcard:

Darling Molly – one day you and I will let them all OUT but meanwhile I am keeping them as comfy as possible, love Caddy.

Molly laminated that postcard so that it would last for ever and carried it around in her school bag until Mr Spencer came across it one day. And smiled.

Sniff, sniff, went Molly, plodding beside me – pathetic, difficult-to-ignore kind of sniffs.

'Molly . . .' I said.

'Stop *asking*!' said Molly. 'Can't you talk about something else?'

So I tried to think of something else. Caddy? No. Vanished. Mr Spencer? No. Terrible. And unfortunately not vanished. David Attenborough (whose laminated autograph Molly also possesses)? Yes. Wonderful. (Always supposing he is still alive.)

'What do you mean?' squealed Molly. 'Rose! Of course he is still alive! Why wouldn't he be, why shouldn't he be? You are horrible!'

Oh dear. Calm down, Mollipop.

'Anyway,' said Mollipop, calming down, 'if he *wasn't* still . . . If he *was* . . . I'm not even going to say it! They'd tell us in Assembly, like if the Queen dies, you know they would.'

How strange is that? For me Assembly is a chance for a ten-minute doze. For Kai it is an opportunity to get his shoes on the right feet. But for Molly it is:

Celebrity Deaths!

I was extremely relieved when Kiran came charging up behind us. Kiran was very bouncy because of her victory over Mr Spencer and she guessed immediately what was making Molly so dismal.

'It's your worst thing ever, isn't it?' she asked, and

without waiting for an answer began recounting some of her and my worst things ever.

And some of them were pretty bad.

Kiran is a wonderful storyteller. She tells stories like some people paint pictures, sketching in the bare facts and then adding details as bright and alive as if they had just been picked from a new box of colours.

Today's story was the account of what happened when Kiran got bored when left alone for five minutes in her father's brand-new parked car. It was very exciting although the only thing Kiran actually did was take off the handbrake. But on a rather steep hill. And when the car began to move, instead of pulling the brake on again, Kiran panicked and jumped out. So the car rolled and rolled, away down the hill, gathering speed, bashing off wing mirrors, frightening old ladies, hitting notices and posts like skittles, faster than anyone could run, keeping stubbornly straight when the road curved, across the pavement and through the automatic opening doors of the Post Office and into the passport photo booth.

Where it stopped.

'*Kiran!*' exclaimed Molly, much cheered.

'But at least I didn't do it *on purpose*,' said Kiran. 'Not like (she won't mind me telling you because she's given it

10

up) when Rose was an actual shoplifter.'

(Oh, thank you very much, Kiran, for digging that one up.)

'*Rose!*'

For a moment Molly actually stopped walking. Then she shrugged and sighed and carried on again. Saying, 'Yes, well, I know shoplifting is illegal and so is smashing a car into the Post Office (I expect) but at least you've never *killed* anyone.'

!!!!!

!!!!!

!!!!!

'Yet,' added Molly fairly.

And Kiran and I were forced to admit that as far as we knew, we hadn't.

After that we walked along very thoughtfully for a while, looking at Molly out of the corners of our eyes now and then, wanting to ask who, and when, and what she had done with the corpse.

Sometimes things are disappointing that should not be disappointing.

The sniffing began again.

I wouldn't call the accidental freeing of Molly's

11

grandma's ancient budgie murder, even if it was discovered ten days later in the jaws of a neighbour's cat.

But poor Molly did.

And none of Kiran's persuasive powers could make her consider that ten days of freedom ending in a cat might be a good exchange for an unlimited future in a very small cage.

Until, just as Molly was about to turn in at the gate of her home, Kiran demanded, 'Which would *you* choose then, the days or the cage?'

'Oh,' said Molly, suddenly transformed, 'oh, the days, the days, the days!'

After Molly left us, Kiran and I walked on together to my house.

At first it seemed that there was no one home. All the windows were dark (I love it when I come home and all the windows are bright) but then we bumped into Mummy outside the back door. She was wearing a sleeping bag like a toga and clutching a hot-water bottle and obviously heading for the garden shed where she paints her pictures, makes private shed-based plans for world peace, and escapes from us, her wonderful family (this time represented by Me).

Kiran and Mummy have met before, so I did not have to explain them to each other.

'Hello, Mrs Casson!' said Kiran.

'Kiran . . . (*sneeze*) how lovely . . . (*sneeze*) Call me . . . (*sneeze*) Eve, darling,' said my mother, her face muffled in a handful of kitchen roll as she backed away like mad. 'Rose, I won't kiss you because I think I may have caught something (*sneeze-gasp-sneeze*). I am going to go and have it in private in the shed . . . (*sneeze*).'

'Oh!'

'One huge germ,' continued Mummy, pointing to her head to make things quite clear. 'So off I go! Hope you had a lovely day at . . .' (she sneezed so hugely that the sleeping bag fell around her knees) '. . . school?'

'No,' I said. 'It was terrible. I've told you before. It gets awfuller every day.'

But I don't think Mummy heard. She was concentrating on recapturing the sleeping bag. Saffy heard instead. She came out of the house just in time. Saffy is my other sister (i.e. the one who is not Caddy). Saffron: seventeen, stunningly beautiful, super-intelligent, and not to be argued with.

'What gets awfuller every day?' she demanded, herding Kiran and me into the kitchen and then rushing about collecting things for Extra Spanish which she does after school two days each week because she is so brainy. 'You're not ill too, are you, Rose? Perhaps you should go and live with Mummy in the shed. Indigo and I could leave you supplies at the door as if you had the plague. Don't look like that, Kiran! She would love it!'

Yes I would.

No school.

It was a wonderful idea and I was about to start fake sneezing straight away when Kiran said, 'She isn't ill at all. It is Mr Spencer that gets more awful every day.'

'Never heard of him,' said Saffron, with her head in her bag.

'Our new class teacher. He doesn't like any of us. Do you know what he said to me last week? He said, "Kiran, you will undoubtedly find yourself in well justified but colossal trouble one day if you do not learn to understand the vital difference between plain fact and paparazzi-style fantasy!" That's what Mr Spencer said. I wrote it down.'

'Tell him less is more when it comes to adjectives,' said Saffron, sounding very uninterested. 'And pass me that blue file, please!'

'He says we are all immature,' continued Kiran (passing it). 'And he says however will Rose manage at Big School in less than one year's time if she cannot read!'

By this time Sarah, Saffron's best friend, had arrived

because she does Extra Spanish too. Sarah has a wheelchair that she uses for transport, emotional blackmail in queues, as an occasional weapon, and as a convenient place to hug people from. I got a quick, protective wheelchair hug as she exclaimed, 'Of course Rose can read! What's the man talking about?'

'Books,' explained Kiran.

'Books?'

'You know how Rose doesn't read books? Mr Spencer can't take it. She stares out of the window and it makes him so mad he—'

'*I* didn't know Rose didn't read books,' interrupted Sarah. 'What, never, Rose? Not even at school?'

'Lazy little disgrace!' remarked Saffron.

'You don't know how it is at our school!' I said, defending myself. 'If you finish one book, they make you pick another. And as soon as you finish that, they send you off again. And each book is a little bit harder than the one before. It's just like a story Indigo once told me about a dragon with two heads. And when the dragon's two heads were cut off, it grew four. And when they were cut off it grew eight . . .'

'I've never *heard* such rubbish!' said Saffron.

'It's true! Do you know what happened when Kiran

finished all the books in the school library last year? They got extra money from the PTA and ordered two hundred more!'

'Actually I was pleased . . .' murmured Kiran.

'So at school now I just . . .'

'Hand over your school bag!' ordered Saffron.

'. . . usually . . .'

Saffron turned my bag upside down and grabbed a book from the heap of junk that fell out.

'. . . draw.'

But Saffy wasn't listening. She was asking, 'What's this supposed to be? Look, Sarah! What does that awful writing say?'

'History,' said Kiran helpfully, craning to look as Saffron flipped through the pages of my history exercise book.

'It's all pictures!' said Sarah, staring at it. 'Hardly any writing at all. How do you get away with it, Rose? Give me another! What's this?'

'Science.'

'*It's* all pictures as well! Where's your Maths?'

'Maths?'

'Maths! Numbers! Sums!'

'Probably at school,' I said.

'Ha!' said Saffron. 'I bet it's all pictures too!'

(A bad guess, although I did not say so. M…
is all Spaces for Missing Work.)

Sarah was looking at me in a truly shocked kind of way.

'Well, I'm with Mr Spencer,' said Saffron, bundling all my stuff back together into my bag and handing it to me. '*I* don't know what you're going to do when you start Big School either! Just don't let on you're related to me. We're late, come on, Sarah!'

Slam.

Saffron was gone.

'Rose,' said Sarah, 'not reading's *awful.*'

It's not.

'You've got to change.'

I don't see why.

'I'll help.'

You needn't.

'Don't argue, I'm *going* to,' said Sarah.

Slam.

Oh.

Kiran left almost straight after Saffy. She was late too. There are always loads of people at Kiran's house, waiting for her to come home and wondering where she is. I can remember when it was like that here. The kitchen used to was never enough space.

there is plenty of space now; a whole houseful.

Where have we all gone?

Mummy is in the shed.

Daddy is in London, being an artist. He says he is getting old.

Caddy, my grown-up sister, has been very elusive for the last year or so. Last heard of in Greece, working in a diving centre, getting up campaigns to rescue unhappy parrots from unsuitable owners, and trying to get over Michael who was the boyfriend she only fell completely in love with after she had agreed to marry someone else.

Michael is avoiding us. I saw him only the other day, teaching someone to drive.

He looked away. Which is not fair, because if anyone was on Michael's side, it was me. Think what I did at Caddy's wedding. (No, don't.)

Saffron. Saffron is on her way to Spanish class.

Indigo, my brother, will be at the music shop in town. He has free guitar lessons from the owner in return for vacuuming the carpets and washing up the day's supply of dirty mugs in the little kitchen at the back.

And

The hamsters all escaped.

The guinea pigs have been given away.

Caddy's wedding rabbit has gone to live with the other rabbits in the petting farm at the zoo.

So that is why

This house

Feels so

Empty.

It Is Dark Because the Clocks Have Changed

I didn't really notice the dark until I got back from school today. Then the house felt very lonely with only me, until I remembered Mummy in the shed. I thought I would make her a cup of tea, but when I took it out to her I found that she was fast asleep, curled up on the old pink sofa that she keeps in there.

Mummy looked nice and warm, but I was cold so I went back into the house and drank her tea.

After that I got out my charcoal and some paper and spread it all out on the living-room floor. I had a new box of charcoal that I had been saving for ages for a really special time. This evening I suddenly realized that this was a ridiculous thing to do. Because when a special time came I would obviously be much too busy (with everyone about and all the excitement and everything) to want to draw at all.

My charcoal is made of willow sticks. It is a dark silvery-grey colour. The sticks are so light that you cannot feel the weight of them in your hand, but they are solid too. Think of an airy dusty metal. A stick of charcoal is a bit like metal. It rings with a thin metal note when you tap it on wood or stone. The sound of it drawing on paper is like a rustle. Like an echo of leaves. If you look carefully at a stick of charcoal you can see where the leaves once hung; they have left patterns like grains of sand, as if a minute bubble burst there and left its shell behind.

It is lovely stuff to draw with. You can layer it into darkness, or brush it away like a dream. You feel like you are drawing with shadows.

The living room was full of shadows.

I always used to be in everyone's way. They would moan about my stuff and step over me and say things like, 'Do you really need to be right there, Rose?' or 'I hope this is going to wash off!' Sometimes they said, 'Show us what you've done!' and fetched each other to come and see and argued about whether it looked right or not.

I used to get interrupted all the time.

I was very glad when my brother Indigo came in. Indigo usually does not get home until much later. Most days he stays in town at school or at the music shop until it is time to do his paper round. It saves him having to go back out again as soon as he has come home.

But today Indigo came back and I was so pleased I jumped up and hugged him.

'I thought you might be on your own,' he said, stepping over my drawing paper to get to the empty fireplace. 'So I came back to make you a fire. David hasn't been round here, has he?'

David is Indigo's friend. He plays the drums quite badly and that is the most interesting thing about him. He hadn't been around, and I said so.

'Sure?' asked Indigo.

I said of course I was. David is not a person it is difficult to spot. He is the height of a Christmas tree and by the way Advent begins tomorrow and I think I am the only person in my family who has noticed this very important fact.

'You'll get presents,' said Indigo, when I mentioned it.

Presents! I was not thinking about presents! I was thinking about *Christmas*.

But Indigo wasn't. He was thinking about David. 'I'm a bit bothered about him,' he said. 'Someone said he was looking for me. I haven't seen him for a while. I'll try and ring him later. Where's Mum? Working?'

'Asleep,' I told him. 'I think she may still be feeling ill from yesterday. She probably hasn't even seen that it's night.'

'It isn't *night*,' said Indigo, grinning. 'It's only dark because the clocks have changed.'

The clocks have changed????

'Weeks ago,' said Indigo. 'Have you only just noticed?'

How had the clocks been changed?

And who had done it?

And who had agreed that they could?

And why, since this new dark was so lonely and early and useless and black, could the clocks not immediately be changed back to their old summery ways?

I asked.

'Hmmm?' said Indigo, raking the ashes down through the grate with the poker, adding a layer of coal, rolling newspaper into empty balls, arranging criss-crossed triangles of kindling, balancing more fuel delicately among the sticks, lighting a corner of paper and beginning to blow. 'What's that, Rosy Pose?'

Nothing.

Lighting a fire without firelighters isn't easy, especially in windy weather when the gusts puff smoke back down the chimney and into the room. The first flames are fragile; little yellow ghosts of warmth. The first red embers are delicate, uncertain things. You have to blow gently on them to make them stay. You have to breathe them into life.

Indigo is good at this. After a minute or two he sat back on his heels, rubbed smoke out of his eyes and said, 'There, it's burning now! Company for you.'

He was in a rush. Already he was pulling on his old grey jacket again and feeling in the pocket for the hat that Sarah had knitted him. Indigo is always busy. His evening paper round takes him more than an hour and he has homework to do too. And I knew he wanted to ring David, and he would probably like to drop in and see Sarah for a bit, and have something to eat and say hello to Mum in her shed. He had all these things to do, but he had taken time to come home and build a fire for me.

So it was not a fair time to make any sort of fuss about being left alone.

Anyway, he really did have to go.

'All right, Rosy Pose?' he asked, already at the door.

So I said, 'Yes, I'm perfectly all right and the fire is brilliant. It's lovely having a fire all to myself.'

'I'm off then,' he said, and went so quickly that he was outside with his bike before I caught him up.

'I'll make you a really good sandwich when you come back,' I said, grabbing his sleeve.

'Good-oh.'

'What'll I put in it?'

24

'Anythi . . .' began Indigo, wheeling his bike round the corner of the house, so I had to run to keep up. Then he looked at my hand, still holding his sleeve. 'I'd like one of those double sandwiches,' he said. 'You know, three slices of bread, one on each side and one in the middle. And I'd like cheese and grilled bacon. Careful with the grill. And salad if we've got any, and pickles if we haven't. I don't mind what colour bread, brown or white is fine but I'd rather it wasn't cut into little triangles. Quite big triangles are OK. Now I really, really have to go, Rosy Pose.'

So I let him.

But it is Advent tomorrow. Advent. The first warm spark of the fire. A small shining in the dark. Shield it from the winter wind. Breathe it into life. Soon it will flame into Christmas.

'Advent?' croaked Mummy, from the far side of the kitchen where she had propped herself to supervise my bacon grilling while keeping her germs as far away as possible. 'Are you sure, Rose?'

'Aren't you pleased?'

'Pleased?' groaned Mummy.

'I love it.'

'Darling Rose,' moaned Mummy. '(No, please, I don't

25

want a sandwich. I couldn't. Even though they look wonderful.) Of course I love it too, it's just the vast amount of work I have promised to do before Christmas.'

'Say you can't.'

'Too late, they paid in advance.'

'Give it back.'

'Spent it.'

'Poor Mummy.'

'Actually, I loved spending it, Rosy Pose.'

'What did you buy?'

'Just stuff,' said Mummy, very vaguely indeed. 'Oh wonderful, here's Indigo. I think I might go and lie down.'

'Are you better than yesterday, do you think, or worse?'

'Better,' said Mummy, with her eyes shut, nodding and nodding her head. 'Much better.'

Good.

Friday 1st December

You wouldn't think it was Advent, the way some people I know are behaving.

And . . .

Two Big Problems:

1. Mr Spencer has said No to Christmas

2. When David said, 'Where will I keep my drum kit?' he didn't mean 'Where will I keep my drum kit?'

Big Problem No 1: Mr Spencer Has Said
No to Christmas

I didn't know that it was legal for a teacher to say no to Christmas. Surely Christmas is compulsory?

'Not here in Class 6,' said Mr Spencer, pulling a hair from his moustache and looking at it to see if it was yellow or grey before dropping it on the floor. 'Here in Class 6 we have a great deal of Ground to Make Up.

'A *great deal* of ground to make up,' repeated Mr Spencer.

For a minute I thought he meant we were all going to have to go outside and dig, and I thought, well, that would not be too bad. Any other time of year.

But he did not mean digging; he meant working.

Working, he explained (with a particularly nasty glance at Gold Team, who are now very handily located by the bins) for an exam we have to take next year called SATs. On which, implied Mr Spencer, leaning over his desk, head jutting forward, entire weight of upper body on knuckles, thumbs inward, think of a chimpanzee (and by the way did you know chimpanzees are not quite the vegetarians they pretend to be? Do you know what else they eat? Monkey. Yes. Raw too. Of course. No microwaves in the jungle. Still. Makes you think), on which (to recap, Mr Spencer on the subject of our SATs) the future of the civilized world depends.

When Class 6 heard this news we moaned and complained and we said all the other classes were doing Christmas and it was not fair.

The other classes are having a lovely time. They are chopping up paper like mad, and hanging tinsel in loops over the windows and learning new Christmas songs downloaded from the internet and packing decorated shoe boxes to send to old people in care homes who would never get a decorated shoe box otherwise. And they are doing many other *Blue Peter* style Christmassy things as well.

We told Mr Spencer all this.

Mr Spencer said:

1. Why should people in care homes be cluttered up with shoeboxes full of tat?
2. There is enough noise pollution in this school without adding to it with Christmas-so-called-I-think-not-saccharine-puerile-music.
3. Nor will he be responsible for any fire hazards in the form of decorations.
4. Christmas cards are environmental disasters.
5. Father Christmas/Santa Claus, Rudolph, sugar plum fairies, singing-talking-flying-through-the-air-snowmen are Not True.
6. Turkeys cause food poisoning.
7. *Blue Peter* should be banned.

Instead, said Mr Spencer, still in his unbecoming alpha-male primate position (I learned all this stuff from Caddy years ago), we will concentrate on revising for our coming exams with the full support of the Head.

The initial groaning was very intense, but after it had died down I discovered something truly shocking. Which was that nobody really cared except me. Kiran said, 'Turkeys *do* cause food poisoning. The family next door to us had it last year and we had to do their shopping for them but they didn't want much. Diet lemonade and rich tea biscuits mostly. My brother says turkeys are *meant* to give people food poisoning. He says it is their defence against Christmas and Natural Evolution and one day people will stop eating them for ever and then the turkeys will have won.'

Kiran is a (theoretical) vegetarian. They are not as reasonable as normal people.

But Molly isn't a vegetarian (in fact she eats no vegetables at all except cucumber) and she was nearly as unbothered as Kiran by Mr Spencer's horrible remarks. She was not even upset by item 5, which I thought would devastate her because I know she leaves out vast quantities of stuff on Christmas Eve, not just mince pies and wine, but buckets of water for the reindeer and thermal gloves and books she thinks Santa might like to read.

Not to mention believing that snowmen have magic sparks inside that take them to North Pole heaven when they melt.

But Molly was OK. She just rolled her eyes and hugged herself. She has been hugging herself a lot today. It is because she has had an idea. (She has been bursting with this idea all day, but she won't tell me and Kiran what it is. Only that it is not boring.)

So anyway, neither Molly nor Kiran were a bit interested in coming with me to the Head to complain, and nearly everyone else I asked at break just moaned, 'Oh *Rose*,' and carried on eating crisps. Kai said, 'I see enough of the Head as it is, without going to see him extra.' Molly added, 'I expect complaining to the Head is probably exactly what Mr Spencer *hopes* we will do,' and Kiran said, 'Molly, you are absolutely right.'

So.

I always loved Christmas at school. Christmas at school felt safe. Until now, nothing had ever gone wrong enough to stop it. Nothing has ever gone wrong enough to stop Christmas at home either, but you can't help wondering if one year it will. Especially when it doesn't snow, and Daddy rings from London to say there is *another* party he can't not go to, and the decorations won't stay up and we all know, even though she never says, how much Mummy is dreading the turkey.

I don't even know who will be at our house for Christmas this year.

But Christmas at school was always reliable, one long lovely very crowded very decorated party that went on for days and days.

Until Mr Spencer said No.

I told the lollipop lady about Mr Spencer saying no to Christmas because I had no one else to moan to.

'Cheer up,' said the lollipop lady. 'There are children starving in Africa.'

LIKE THAT IS SUPPOSED TO CHEER ME UP.

Big Problem No 2: When David Said, 'Where Will I Keep My Drum Kit?', He Didn't Mean 'Where Will I Keep My Drum Kit?'

When I got home from school this afternoon I had a big surprise. Our kitchen was full of bags of food. Enough to last for days and days. All my favourite things were there. Honey, tomato soup, tinned meatballs and spaghetti, oaty biscuits and apples. Everything.

Mummy was in the bathroom having a very hot disinfectant bath that smelled right down the stairs.

'I am obliterating germs, Rose darling!' she snuffled through the bathroom door. 'And I'm sure all that food is perfectly safe because I wore disposable gloves and a scarf over my face all the way round the supermarket.'

'Didn't people stare?' I asked.

'Oh well, maybe,' admitted Mummy, splashing a bit. 'Do you think you could unpack for me, Rosy Pose?'

I was very happy to unpack, and I loaded all the food in neat patterns on the store cupboard shelves.

I unpacked: cheese (two large packets of ready grated), apples (twenty-four), honey jars (three), spaghetti and meatball tins (eleven), tomato soup (one four-pack), oaty cookies (four packets), Family Size Farmhouse Fresh Frozen Chicken Pies (three), eggs (two dozen), milk (twelve litres, which took up the whole of the bottom of the freezer), headache tablets (six boxes), paper hankies (six boxes), disinfectant (four large spray bottles), Stayfresh Muffins (forty-eight), instant hot chocolate (two big tubs), pink and white marshmallows (two packets).

From Mummy's shopping I deduced:

1. That she had rushed round the supermarket scooping up whole armloads of the same thing at a time.

2. That she wasn't planning on getting better overnight.

I showed off my unpacking to Mummy when she came downstairs with her head wrapped round in a towel and her nose as red as Rudolph's.

'Now I can stop worrying,' she said, admiring from an uncontaminating distance. 'You won't starve. Will you be all right, darling, if I buzz off to the shed now? I'd love to stay and chat but I don't want to breathe on you too much . . . Horrible if you caught this. Not that it's anything.'

She bent to hug me like she always does, and then remembered and backed away. 'After I'm better I'll hug you twenty times to make up,' she said. 'Meanwhile, back to my stony tower . . . Aren't I lucky so many people want my pictures? Think how I'd worry if they didn't.'

'Like Daddy,' I agreed, because all this year Daddy has remarked how Bad Things Have Become At The Top.

'No, no, no,' said Mummy, 'there is no comparison. Why don't you make yourself some hot chocolate, you used to love it when you were little?'

So, I did, and I put marshmallows on top, enough to melt and make a gooey pink and white marsh with the chocolate oozing through like swamp water. I offered to make some for Mummy too, but she said, 'Please, please, no!' and held her stomach and hurried out to the shed with a fresh box of tissues and a new disinfectant spray.

Poor Mummy.

But at least she was very clean.

I only noticed after she had gone that it was dark again.

I'm not scared of the dark; I just don't like it. I don't like the black reflections it makes in the windows, and I don't like the way it makes sudden noises louder, and I don't like the way it gets into your head, so you think things you wouldn't dream of thinking if it was daylight.

And it stops you wanting to move from room to room.

In case when you are opening the door a face is there, a huge enormous face, right opposite yours, and it shrieks WAAAAAH!!!!!

I just don't like the idea of that.

What I *really* would have liked to do was telephone Kiran, but I couldn't because the phone was in the kitchen and I was in the living room and I don't have my own mobile.

In New York, where my friend Tom lives, it would not be dark at this time. It would only be early afternoon.

When you are on your own you can do things that are not possible at any other time. For instance, you can groan.

I quite like groaning on my own, so I did it for a while, and then I did something I have never done before.

I lit the living-room fire.

By myself.

I copied exactly what Indigo had done, but it took much, much longer, and the room was foggy with smoke and my eyes were very sore before I finally got it going. But it did. And it blazed up properly and started to be warm and I thought how pleased everyone would be when they got home.

I thought this for about one minute.

And then I thought, if Indigo finds out I can light the fire by myself he'll never have to come home and do it for me again.

And then I thought, *Put it out! Put it out! Put it out!*

So then I opened both windows to cool it down with cold outside air but that didn't work, and it roared and smoked in the draught until I pulled them shut again.

After that I poked it all to pieces with the poker and put coal dust on top and the smoke went all chokey but the fire still was not out. So then I forgot the WAAAAH! face and ran into the kitchen for water and I got a whole kettle full of cold and poured that on, and the fire went out then, but it went out hissing like a furious tiger and spitting out little pieces of coal. I trod on one of the spat-out bits of coal and it was red hot and sticking to the carpet and it was a job to get it back into the fire.

But I managed. And I turned off the lights in case there were any more bits because I thought it would be easier to see them glowing in the dark. And it was. While I was there in the dark grovelling round the floor groaning a little bit (because you might as well if it helps), I heard someone bang on our back door.

The back door of our house leads straight into the kitchen. Of course, it wasn't locked. Why should it be

36

locked? It was not really night and Mummy wasn't far away (although far enough. Would she hear, for instance, a scream, out there in her shed? Of course she would).

My immediate thought, when I heard that bang, was to get behind the sofa and pretend there was no one home.

That was what I did, and as soon as I had done it, I heard the back door open.

But I hardly had time to be frightened for a moment, because a blurry voice called, 'Hello! Hello?' and straight away I recognized it.

Bother oh bother oh bother oh bother.

It was David.

Indigo's dopey, huge, kind, not-very-bright and very-easy-to-have-enough-of friend David.

David, who is simultaneously in love with Saffron and Sarah and his drum kit and me.

David, who never, ever knows when it is time to go home.

I was very glad indeed that I had decided to get behind the sofa.

'Hello, hello!' called David again. His voice sounded different somehow; creaky. And then I heard him come into the living room, and of course it must have looked completely empty to him because I was quite well hidden tween the sofa and the wall and there was no light except what came through the open door from the kitchen.

'Oh!' said David, obviously realizing how empty things were, and after that I heard a sort of sob and he plonked down on the sofa so hard it jerked backwards and bumped my head.

Then the sobs grew helplessly worse.

What a strange thing to do, to go to someone's house, and sit in an empty room that is not yours, and make such a noise. I crawled out to have a look.

Poor David. His face was in his dripping hands. He was crying and rubbing away tears, but not as fast as they poured down his big red cheeks. Poor poor David. I tried very hard to make myself care as much as I should. It was very difficult, because he looked such a mess.

'Where'll I keep my drum kit?' he was blubbering, over and over again, and when I appeared before him he did not act a bit surprised, just said, 'Rose, where'll I keep my drum kit. Rose?' and then lost his voice in a great bubbling choke.

Oh dear.

I moved my favourite green cushion out of reach of the flood. Caddy says animals don't cry; they put up with things until they're too unbearable to put up with, and then they die. Humans are the only creatures that truly cry, and

I think they look very nasty doing it. No wonder, I said to myself, looking at David, that Noah concentrated on saving the animals when he built the ark.

Burble, burble, burble, went David, sounding like a plug hole. 'What'll I do? Where'll I keep my drum kit, Rose?'

I just stood there, wishing. I wished Indigo was with me to understand. Or Saffy to shake back her hair and diagnose. Or Mummy to not mind the splashes and the swampy tears, and hug.

But they were not here, and neither was faraway Caddy, who would have cried in sympathy and asked useless questions. Nor Daddy, remarking, 'Tears. Well. Ask not for whom the bell tolls, what's the damage?' feeling for his wallet, and trying not to say, or even think, that all this emotion was very, very exhausting and not exactly art.

There was nobody there except me.

And, of course, poor David.

With his drum kit problem.

'Rose,' squelched David, heaving himself to his feet, sniffing and blotting his face with his sleeve, and still nearly drowning in his own juice, 'when I said "Where'll I put my drum kit?" I didn't mean "Where'll I put my drum kit?" Do you understand? Do you understand that?'

I cannot cope with everything – Mr Spencer, and Kai,

and Molly's gran's dead budgie, and Christmas and the dark and Mummy in the shed, and Saffron saying not to let on I'm related to her, and Cheer up Rose, there are children starving in Africa, and *now David, too.*

'Do you understand, Rose?' asked David, very wetly indeed.

So I said NO.

Saturday 2nd December

Three things that I found out this morning:

1. Saffron and Sarah will be checking up on me (Saffy).
2. Aromatherapy is a wonderful thing.
3. When Molly said, 'Promise you will help, please promise you will help!' Kiran and I should not have said, 'Of course we will!' We should have said, 'Help you with what?'

Saffron and Sarah Will Be Checking Up On Me

I woke up this morning thinking Oh I Cannot Bear Another Day of School and then I realized it was Saturday and I didn't have to.

That is the nicest way to wake up.

The house was so quiet that I thought everyone must be asleep, but when I tiptoed out to do a bed inspection I found the rooms were all empty. So I stopped being unselfishly quiet and went downstairs as noisily as I liked.

There were three notes on the kitchen table:

Darling Rose – I have gone to Boots for something to inhale. Back Very Soon, Love Mummy
PS Don't go anywhere. PS again. The funny smell is disinfectant spray so you are quite safe.

Rose, stay where you are. Sarah and I will be checking up on you, X Saffy

Rosy Pose, please hang on here in case David turns up because I haven't seen him for a week, Indigo
AND IF HE DOES TURN UP BE NICE!!!

So there I was, protected, organized, threatened and obviously not going anywhere.

My family are always leaving me messages telling me not to go anywhere. Saffy says it is because if I stay put at home, then everyone knows where I am. They like to know where I am. Saffy says they don't want always to

41

have to be wondering, 'Where is Rose?'

This isn't fair. I like to know where they are, and if they'd stayed put at home I would not always have to be wondering, 'Where is everyone?'

I grumbled a bit about all this in my head while I went on a breakfast hunt for anything except cereal because only Daddy can make me eat cereal (unless it's porridge). There was no bread but that did not matter because there are still forty-six muffins left, no one being very keen on muffins here except me. I did offer one to David last night, but he just shook his head and said 'No, no, no' and gathered himself up to leave, making me feel glad and guilty at the same time. Mostly glad, and I was able to get rid of the guilt by giving him a handkerchief with a pink rose in the corner to use to dab his eyes (I have a whole lot of rose handkerchiefs that I keep specially for crying with. I like to cry on something proper. It feels so sad and interesting, dabbing your eyes on a real white hanky. But they are no good for noses). I gave David the downstairs toilet roll for his nose (Economy Peach).

As well as muffins I found half a box of breadsticks, three fun-sized Mars bars, two bananas and Saffy's mobile phone. I carried all this back upstairs with me and had a very nice breakfast and then I texted Kiran (who was also in bed) and we began to play a game where we go pretend Christmas shopping with a million pounds each and every time we think of something new to buy we text each other to see what they think.

The first thing I bought was for Molly. It was a painted gypsy caravan with two nice grey donkeys to pull it. Molly hasn't had any pets since her cat Buttons got squashed. Her mother said never again, too draining, no more pets allowed ever because Molly was so upset she had to have two weeks off school (which is longer than you get for the death of a near relative) but I do not think that donkeys count as pets. No one has said Molly is not allowed transport.

Kiran thought the gypsy caravan was a very good present and would probably cost around nine hundred pounds (five hundred for the caravan and two hundred each for the donkeys). So then I had one million take nine hundred pounds left and I sent Kiran a text to ask how much that was.

Straight away she sent one back saying: **u hv 999100 i hv bort Mr S sm v glam yot wiv rmt contr 0 in btm wich we cn activ8 mid Oshun wot do u fink**

I think it is a brilliant idea! Mr Spencer will never be able to resist the temptation of a small very glamorous yacht. But how would we be able to tell when he was mid ocean?

It would be a waste to activate the hole within swimming distance of land.

Kiran had the same worries, but she thought of a way to manage that sounded like it would work although it was not cheap.

we wil hv 2 helicoptr monitr, Kiran wrote. **wil u go 1/2s? u hv 499100 1ft if so cos I thk approx cost helicoptr 1000000.**

A million pounds! Goodness! Still, probably worth it to have Mr Spencer sunk mid ocean (and I suppose we would also have a helicopter to do what we liked with afterwards). But I didn't get a chance to agree because it was just then that Saffron and Sarah pounced into my room without knocking and started checking up on me (as threatened).

'We knew you would still be in bed!' they said to me. 'We've already been for a swim. Look at the crumbs and Mars wrappers! What are you doing? Whose phone have you nicked? Move up so we can sit down!'

So I did and they did, Sarah on my feet and Saffy on a concealed banana.

'Stop laughing, Rose!' ordered Sarah, while Saffy picked ruined banana from her best Gap jeans. 'This is serious. We've come all the way back here just to bring you a book.'

'I can't *read* books,' I protested. 'You know I can't!'

'You've been trying the wrong sort,' said Sarah. '*I* brought you this!'

Then she dropped on my legs a thing like a slab of concrete. 'Gombrich. *The Story of Art*,' she said smugly. 'Perfect for you! Nothing like any school reading book you've ever seen and it's full of stuff about people who draw on walls like you. It's even got pictures, so get on with it.'

'She never will,' said Saffron.

'She will.'

Sarah is sixteen, nearly seventeen. She has a white face and dark eyes and black hair swinging in two points against her cheeks.

'*Here lies,*' she said, patting the bump my legs made under the quilt, '*poor Rose.*

'*Illiterate from head to toes.*'

'Dope,' said Saffy, smiling at her.

Soon after that they left, calling and laughing, flicking open tiny mirrors, pushing things in bags, scattering down the stairs and out of the back door.

'Where are you going *now?*' I asked, rolling out of bed at the last minute to rush downstairs and shiver on the doorstep in my pyjamas.

'Oh,' they said. 'Out. Town. Shops. Library. Get inside before you freeze!'

But I stayed to watch them go, Sarah waving from her wheelchair under a heap of bags and scarves and both their jackets, Saffron in her slightly banana-y jeans.

Saffy's hair made a blowing brightness in the grey of the street.

Gone.

Aromatherapy Is a Wonderful Thing

I ran away once, to London. I didn't mean to; I just got stuck in a train that was going that way. And I ended up in New York (where it will still be dark right now). (New York is where Tom lives.) London is where Daddy lives. It used to be his favourite place, but I don't think it is any more. Daddy is Burned Out. He told me so last week. And London is losing its magic (says Daddy).

I never knew it had any. I did not notice any magic when I was there. The only thing I really saw (apart from people and traffic) was scaffolding. Huge buildings held up by scaffolding.

Not very magical.

Daddy liked London too much to see the scaffolding.

He had a lovely girlfriend there called Samantha, and a nice lady to clean his flat, and loads of friends, and he could visit Mummy and Caddy and Indigo and Saffy and me whenever he liked just by hopping on a train. Which was much easier than having to actually live with us. Because we put him off his Art.

Good thing we don't put Mummy off her Art too, or else we would be orphans.

Artistic orphans.

Luckily Mummy is the opposite to Daddy. She doesn't think London is magic and she needs us very much, Caddy and Saffron and Indigo and me. We are her best thing in the world. She would never paint another brushstroke if it wasn't for us; she actually said that, not very long ago. We are her inspirations. And so are the bills.

Soon after Saffron and Sarah left, Mummy came back from her trip to Boots, so I got dressed as quickly as I could and went out to the shed to see how she was getting on.

She was getting on very well. She had brought back a bagful of little bottles and the air was fantastically alive with lavender and tea tree and eucalyptus and rosemary and basil. You would not believe such an enormous smell could come out of such tiny bottles. I did not know flowers could be so strong, my eyes felt quite stingy from them.

'Now it is just a matter of waiting for it to work,' said Mum through the germ-proof hanky she was holding over her face like a mask. 'Aromatherapy! Isn't it gorgeous? Goodness, my head!'

'What is the matter with your head?' I asked.

'Oh nothing, nothing,' she said, squirting disinfectant spray into the air between us, her eyes very bright over the top of the hanky. 'Lovely and floaty, Rose darling. Just right. I am feeling so well already.'

She did look better. Her cheeks were pink and she had stopped sneezing completely, which was a good job because you cannot sneeze and draw at the same time. She'd been drawing when I arrived, a picture of St Matthew's Church.

Mummy has done a lot of churches this year, pen and ink sketches painted in afterwards with sploshy water-colours like pictures in a colouring book. Nearly always there are people in the picture, tiny groups in the church porch. They have not caught on for funerals (can't think why) but are very popular for christenings and weddings.

An Original Work of Art, and a Personal Memory of Your Most Special Day

People buy them in bulk for weddings, one each for the bridesmaids, one for the bride's parents, one for the groom's, one for Great-Granny because she is very old and might not make it to another Big Day . . . The tiny figures in the porch (sketched from photographs) shuffle into new positions depending on who will be getting the picture. One moment poor old Granny is centre stage, the next the Littlest Bridesmaid. Sometimes, for a surprise to the bride, an extra guest is painted in who never actually made it on the day (hurray, hurray it is Gandalf/Madonna/the cat!).

The skies are what you notice most. The skies and the mounts. Pinkish skies in pink mounts, pale blue skies in pale blue mounts, golden in golden.

I am sorry to say that Mummy colours the skies to match the bridesmaids' dresses.

Once someone had multicoloured bridesmaids.

So Mummy created a rainbow.

The picture on the drawing board today was of St Matthew's in the marketplace. That's the church where my sister Caddy once nearly got married, except that at the last minute she was saved. ('For another fate' as Saffron remarked at the time.) And so the wedding didn't end as well as it had started. However, other people do manage to get married quite successfully in St Matthew's. Mummy often has to draw it. (She's got very good at reducing the huge looming gravestones which pack the churchyard in all ~~their~~ dabbled glow.)

Recently a very large family had had a wedding there, very successfully indeed, and they ordered and paid for a huge number of works of art to commemorate the day with all different combinations of bridesmaids, cats, old grannies etc. centre stage. And they wanted all these masterpieces painted, framed, packed and delivered by Christmas, when they would be handed out at a family mass reunion from under the Christmas tree.

So poor old Mummy was slaving away like mad.

Today's St Matthew's was not Mummy's usual style at all. There was something terribly exciting about the steeple. It was whizzing backwards into space like a rocket.

It was magnificent; it made me giddy, just looking at it.

'It is your best St Matthew's ever,' I told Mummy.

'Is it?' asked Mummy, sounding very surprised and twisting the drawing board about a bit to try and see what I meant.

'Stand back and you will see properly,' I suggested, so Mummy pushed back her hair and got to her feet to have a look herself.

'See?' I said. 'Isn't it brilliant?'

Mummy swayed around, admiring the brilliantness. Then she said, 'Lost my vanishing point,' in a very surprised voice, and lay down suddenly on h

So I said, 'Mummy?'

For a little while Mummy did not reply. Then she said, 'Aromatherapy is a wonderful thing,' and sat up, and staggered back across to St Matthew's again.

'I shall have to redraw,' she said, after blinking at it for a bit. 'And I can't even begin to think of the colours. The bridesmaids wore jade green with white lace . . . What are you planning to do this morning?'

'Kiran said could I go round to her house?'

'Of course you can.'

'Are you going to paint a jade-green sky?'

'I don't see why I shouldn't,' said Mummy, inhaling neat lavender and tea tree, one bottle to each nostril in a slightly cross kind of way. 'I've been asked to slim down the bridesmaids, and pump up the groom and work in a hunky footballer for Granny, so I don't see why I shouldn't have a jade-green sky. And don't look so shocked, Rosy Pose! After all, we both know, this is not exactly Art!'

I can't believe Mummy said that.

When Molly Said, 'Promise You Will Help, Please Promise You Will Help!' Kiran and I Shouldn't Have Said, 'Of Course We Will!', We Should Have Said, 'Help You With What?'

Anyway, I went to Kiran's house.

Molly was there. Molly, with her long straight no-coloured hair in a very tight ponytail, freshly ironed Saturday jeans, anorak, Barbie pink trainers and library ticket. Molly, with her anxious eyes, list of emergency phone numbers and chewed finger ends. She and Kiran were messing about in Kiran's front garden when I arrived, waiting for me. I saw at once that Kiran was in a lovely silly mood and Molly wasn't.

'Kiran,' said Molly to me, 'thinks I'm boring.'

'I never said that!' said Kiran, hanging herself by her knees from a thickish branch of the lilac tree by the gate. 'Push me, someone!'

I pushed her gently in the stomach so she swung like washing.

'You're getting tree-green on your jeans,' Molly remarked. *'And* we can see your underwear.'

'You can't!' said Kiran.

'We can!'

52

'*Which* underwear?'

'The whole of the tops of your socks,' said Molly, 'are showing. Aren't they, Rose?'

Um. Yes.

'Socks aren't underwear,' said Kiran. 'Are they, Rose?'

Um. No.

'*Say* something, Rose!' said Molly and Kiran.

So I told them that they were both right, Kiran's socks were showing, but socks weren't underwear, and I gave Kiran an extra hard shove to create a diversion.

'Oh, this is bliss,' said Kiran happily. 'I can see lovely floating silver stars. Can anybody else?'

Then she went smashing to the ground.

'Silver stars, looping round and round,' said Kiran, showing no emotion at her sudden change in position. 'I've got a wonderful blurry feeling too. It is better than being drunk.'

'Lie still in case you've broken your back,' said Molly. 'We did it in the Brownies. Socks are underwear, why do you think everyone keeps them in their underwear drawers and I didn't say you said I was boring, Kiran. I just said you thought it. And I expect Rose thinks I am too. And so does everyone . . .' (Molly paused to cry two round shiny tears.) 'Can you move your arms and legs?' she continued. 'Can you turn your head? You may have concussion. I should wrap you in a space blanket but I don't see what good it would do.'

The tears splashed on to her anorak.

'It's washable,' she said. 'At forty degrees.'

Then all three of us laughed so much it hurt.

'Bonkers,' said Kiran, flat out in the place where there are daffodils when it is daffodil time (not now). 'Mollipop's gone bonkers. What do you think, Rose?'

I said I thought we should all hang upside down because the stars sounded so good and I hoped they would be visible to someone like me who could only usually see stars with glasses. And at night.

So we did. And you could. Even with your eyes shut you could see those stars. Also we could hear the sea thumping in our heads. I said, 'We should do this always, every day. Like owls . . .'

'Bats,' said Kiran. 'And not day. Night.'

'Owls. They cough up bones . . . My stars leave trails, like sparklers do on firework night . . .'

'My stars . . .' began Kiran, and then slipped off again, and I fell too, from watching her.

'. . . are fizzy,' said Kiran. 'Fizzy stars . . . are you all right up there, Mollipop?'

54

I looked at Molly too. She was quite silent, upside down in her clean jeans, with her arms tidily folded and her feet crossed so the top of her socks didn't show.

'Are you my friends?' asked Molly.

'You know we are,' answered Kiran and I.

'Proper friends?'

'Yes, yes,' we said a bit crossly, because she sounded so doubtful.

'There is this one thing that I've always wanted to do . . .'

Kiran and I waited.

'I *am* boring,' said Molly. 'I knew I was.'

We on the ground made moaning noises.

'If I wasn't I would do it . . .'

Molly is quite able to twitter on like this for hours and hours and hours, round and round a decision she cannot make, or a secret she dare not tell. She sometimes needs a decision-maker. You could see she was relieved when Kiran helped her out.

'Do it!' ordered Kiran, addressing Molly's upside-down head in a very bossy voice. 'Whatever it is, do it! You must, mustn't she, Rose?'

I said I didn't know.

'Come on, Rose,' whispered Kiran. 'It can't be that bad! It's only a Molly-idea.'

Kiran said afterwards that she did not think Molly would hear her, being upside down. But of course Molly did.

'Oh,' she said, and cried a tear or two more. They ran up her forehead and got lost in her fringe.

'I thought you were my friends,' she snuffled.

'We are, we are,' we groaned. 'Stop it, Moll!'

'I want to do it.'

'Good,' we said. 'Good. Do it! Brilliant! Not boring at all! Do you want us to help?'

'Yes, but you wouldn't,' snuffled Molly.

'Of course we would!'

'Promise?' asked Molly, suddenly flipping off her branch and standing over us pink-faced, eyes gleaming, fists in tight balls. 'Promise you'll help! *Truly* promise you'll help!'

'Of *course* we will!' we said.

'*Absolutely* we will,' we repeated (foolishly).

Not, Help you with what?

56

Sunday 3rd December

I had two phone calls today. They were from Daddy and Caddy.

That is the first time I have noticed that Daddy and Caddy rhyme. I could make a poem out of that if I wanted.

Only I don't.

The first thing Daddy said was, 'You are quite right, Rose! There is scaffolding everywhere . . .'

'I told you so!'

'I know you did. How are things at home?'

Things were fine, I said, much tidier than the last time he was here (Daddy likes things very tidy). Saffron and Indigo were at Sarah's house having a Homework Mass Attack to which I also had been invited (No thank you. I will turn up some time much nearer lunch) and Mummy was very busy with a DARLINGS DO NOT DISTURB notice on the shed door. The shed itself smelled wonderfully of lavender and tea tree and 99.9 Per Cent Effective in 30 Seconds disinfectant spray, and that was all the news.

'Disinfectant spray?' repeated Daddy. 'Is Eve ill?'

'She had a cold,' I told him. 'But she is getting better every minute.'

'What's she doing now?' he asked.

'Oh,' I said. 'Working, I suppose. She has a lot of churches to draw and she says she's lost her vanishing point.'

'Lost her *what*?' he demanded. 'Rose? Rose, are you still there, Rose?'

I had forgotten Daddy for a moment, because out of the window I had seen a surprising sight. David. Lumbering down the road towards our house, lurching from side to side like it was all he could do to stay upright. And whatever had happened to him? David had always been large, but now he looked immense. He had doubled in size overnight.

I hardly ever wear my glasses, because in my opinion the world looks better slightly blurred, but now I reached them out of the cupboard where they live behind the jam, dusted them off, and had a look.

David hadn't doubled in size. He was carrying a drum kit.

'Rose!' yelled Daddy down the phone, very cross that I had suddenly abandoned him.

So I had to talk a bit longer about Mummy and vanishing points and he kept saying, 'How *exactly* did she say it? Was it a joke? You must have noticed if it was a joke! Did she mention anything else? Did she mention me at all? What did she *mean*?'

...how it was humanly possible to carry a whole drum kit, and I watched until David came close enough for me to see how it was done.

Very disappointing. He had it in a wheelbarrow. And, very alarmingly, he was getting along quite quickly. Soon he would arrive at our back door, and then I would be STUCK.

So I said, 'Sorry, darling Daddy, got to go,' and put the phone down and rushed upstairs and didn't answer the doorbell which made me feel very mean.

Poor old David. He did look gloomy walking away.

But perhaps he was only busking.

Caddy!

Amazing!

It is *months* since we heard from Caddy; Saffy was the last person to speak to her and she wrecked it right from the start by saying, 'Caddy! Where are you? Are you all right? What are you doing? Did you ever find Michael and have you had a row because he is back in town doing his driving lessons again and he goes around looking like thunder and won't speak to any of us and it really upsets Rose?'

'Absolutely typical of this family,' said Caddy. 'You call

59

to say hello and before you know it you are up to your neck in emotional blackmail and third-degree cross-questioning. *Goodbye!*'

For months after that we had a sticker on the phone saying: DON'T ASK CADDY ANYTHING.

It peeled off long ago, but the faint sticky mark it left was enough to remind me to be very careful. So I said, 'Hi Caddy . . .' (as if I'd spoken to her only yesterday instead of a year ago) '. . . I've just not answered the door to David. He came round with his drum kit in a wheelbarrow. What do you think?'

'What size wheelbarrow?' asked Caddy, sounding so bouncy and interested she might have been just up the road.

'Very small. You could hardly see it under all the drums.'

'I wonder if he was busking,' said Caddy. 'Perhaps he wanted Indigo to help. I hope not. It isn't exactly busking weather.'

'What's busking weather?'

'Well, summer,' said Caddy, laughing.

(*Hurray*, I thought. *She is laughing. I am getting on brilliantly.* And I began to listen out for clues to where she might be.)

'Perhaps David thinks it's late summer. Very, very, very, late summer.'

'Well, it's not,' said Caddy. 'It's winter!' (*Ah ha! So she's in the Northern hemisphere! Now to narrow it down!*)

'Do you think it's too early in the day to ring Tom in New York?'

'Much too early! They'll not even be awake yet. In fact, I bet it's still dark over there.'

(So, Northern hemisphere, but not America.)

'Are you missing Tom, Rosy Pose?' asked Caddy.

'I am always missing Tom,' I said, before I thought, and then I said, 'Don't tell anyone I said that, Caddy! Caddy, promise you won't!'

'Relax, Rose,' said Caddy, very kindly. 'Everyone knows you don't care a bit!'

'Do they? Do you think Tom thinks that?'

'NO!' said Caddy. 'I was teasing! I'm sorry. I shouldn't have. Tell me about school.'

(Listen! Caddy is obviously on location at some wildlife park. There is definitely an animalish background noise. Squeals and snuffles and grunts and wails. Hungry animals, by the sound of it too. I hoped Caddy hadn't noticed them, because she is very soft-hearted about starving animals, and now that I'd got her talking I wanted her to stay for a while. Not rush off and start dealing out lunch.)

At first I didn't know where to begin telling Caddy about

school. So much has changed since I last saw her. However, once I got started I enjoyed myself. I started on a super big moan about Mr Spencer and it was brilliant because it made Caddy groan and laugh and ask silly questions. Caddy said Mr Spencer sounded an ogre and she had never ever had a teacher as terrible as that herself. (I do love it when people say things like that. Instead of saying, as so many do, 'Yes, but if you think that was bad I know something far worse.' And then you have to think of something worse than their something, and it all ends up big lies.) But it was the opposite with Caddy. I don't often get encouraged to go on and on in such an unlimited kind of way but in the end I had to stop. The cries of the starving animals were too furious to ignore.

'Love to everyone,' said Caddy hurriedly. 'Are they all OK?'

'Except for Mummy's cold,' I said. 'Everyone else is fine and it is Sunday Lunch at Sarah's today, we are all going except Mummy. She thought she would rather work. Saffy and Indigo are there already. Sarah's mum is making something called Snow White Christmas Pudding so what do you think that is?'

Caddy said she had no idea, but Sarah's mum's cooking was always superb and she was sure it would be yum.

And then she hurried off to feed the animals and I rushed too, first to tell Mummy that Caddy had re-emerged with practically an address (Wildlife Park, Not America, Northern Hemisphere) and then down the road to Sarah's house with the same good news.

Caddy was right. Sarah's mum's cooking was superb. Only I would have enjoyed it much more if Saffy and Sarah and Indigo had not complained so much at me for not finding out one useful thing about Caddy. Because, unlike Mummy who had been very thrilled, they were not at all impressed at my detective skills and they said the address I had found could be easily shortened to Almost Anywhere.

I had to change the subject by producing (between dinner and pudding) E. H. Gombrich's enormously heavy and tightly bound *The Story of Art*.

'How far did you get?' asked Sarah's mother, and I said that by skipping the preface and the two introductions I had made it to the cavemen which everyone thought very funny indeed.

'Didn't you even flick through and look at the pictures?' asked Sarah.

I said no, because there were too many and Sarah's dad said he completely understood.

'Art galleries have exactly the same effect on me,' he said.

'The only thing I look for in them is the Exit signs. You come with me, Rose, I'll show you a proper picture.'

So I went with him into the hall and admired (for about the hundredth time in my life) Sarah's dad's most favourite picture in all the world. Which is an aerial photograph of a Scottish golf course with him actually in it, wearing a bright red jumper he bought specially to show up.

'Lovely,' he murmured, stroking it lovingly. 'I could have had a Canvas Effect and then it would have looked just like an oil painting but some of the detail would have gone. Mind you, we had to work for it, Rose. Stood there all morning, waiting for the plane! Best spot on the whole course. That's my mate Graham in blue. He had a good place too, but I did better. We tossed for the eighteenth . . . That bit of black by the gorse is my jacket, I took it off you see . . . What's the matter with them in there?'

He meant Sarah's mum and Saffy and Sarah and Indigo, who were all dying with laughter at this Commentary on Art. Because all of us have heard it many, many times before. We love it. It is as good as a bedtime story. Also it goes on for ages (once we encouraged him to keep it up for nearly an hour). However this time we only had the short version because Sarah's mother interrupted by shouting, 'Pudding!'

Snow White Christmas Pudding is absolutely wonderful.

You can eat much more of it than you can of normal Christmas Pudding. But it is only snow white if you don't count the cherries and the chocolate sauce. Sarah's father had three platefuls with extra sauce and then he said it was very pleasant but he could see why it had never caught on.

'You are utterly hopeless,' said Sarah's mother, hitting him with the entire *Sunday Times* (which is twice as big as Gombrich). 'You can load up the dishwasher unaided, and don't you go getting sorry for him, Rose!'

'No I won't,' I said, but afterwards I did sneak into the kitchen to help. Because Sarah's dad is very nice and very funny. And he said he thought I'd done remarkably well with Caddy.

And so did I.

Monday 4th December

Throw the Book Away

I forgot to take my PE kit into school today. This was Mr Spencer's fault for ordering us to take them home at the end of last week and get them properly washed. As if anyone could get their PE kit washed in two days. In our house that sort of job takes all summer.

Kai was not doing PE either because his mother had sent him in with a Note. So we had to sit on a bench together and watch the others do boring things with hoops and mats because Mr Spencer is too lazy to get out the ropes and wall bars and climbing frames. He makes us do Balancing on the Floor.

(Ridiculous.

How does he think we ever learned to walk if we couldn't balance on the floor?

It is not as if there is anywhere to go to if you fall off.)

Kai and I were supposed to be noticing and learning.

So we did.

I did anyway. I noticed how incredibly like each other

all the boys looked from the back, and how Molly pointed her toes naturally as a result of too many ballet lessons, and how Mr Spencer (who was forced to give his orders standing around in socks because our gym floor is a sacred object hardly to be stepped on) left large damp footprints whenever he moved. Which was not very often, I am pleased to say.

Then Kai disturbed my noticing with a furtive remark.

'I feel sick,' he said. 'I've been feeling sick all morning.'

I moved a little further away from him on the bench.

'Mum said it was nothing but a headache and sent me in with a note.'

'Go to the office,' I ordered urgently.

'No,' said Kai. 'Mr Spencer'll never let me. Say things to stop me thinking about it, Rose.'

'Look at Mr Spencer's yuck footprints.'

'I know. They make me feel terrible.'

Oh dear. Not surprising though. I tried again.

'What did you do at the weekend?'

'Watched football.'

'What else?'

'Made a list of the girls I fancied.'

'Is there anyone on it I know?'

''Course,' said Kai. 'All the girls in this class are on it . . .'

Good grief!

'Except you.'

'Why don't you fancy *me*?' I demanded, forgetting to whisper because I was so astonished at this unfairness, and all the people near our corner fell out of their hoops with giggles.

'Har, har, har!' groaned Kai, doubled up with laughter. 'Got you!'

I pushed him backwards off the bench and he hit his head on the wall.

'Rose and Kai!' snapped Mr Spencer from the other side of the room. 'I am watching you!'

So we watched him back, staring meaningfully at his sweaty footprints, but he didn't notice.

Glum silence, broken by Kai who murmured, 'Hit me on my nose.'

'What?'

'Hit me on my nose,' hissed Kai.

'Why?'

'Why not?'

'No!'

'Just do it, Rose!'

'No.'

'You're not scared of Mr Spencer, are you?' taunted Kai, wagging his nose at me.

So I hit it an unenthusiastic swipe and he groaned and grabbed it with both hands.

OH NO!

Red.

A huge blooming patch of blood-red falling from his hands, and the walls of the room closing in around me and a dreadful weird hotness and coldness and lightness. Then darkness. No colour anywhere except for the running, spreading, scarlet . . .

Fainted.

I came round in the office to a voice asking if I had had any breakfast.

Even after they explained that Kai's sanguine catastrophe (Saffy's words. Quoted in admiration) was nothing worse than a Trick Blood-soaked Hanky from the joke shop, breakfast was the last thing I wanted right then. So they rang Mummy to come and fetch me home and she didn't answer. And then they tried Sarah's mother who is my first emergency number, and she wasn't there either. Obviously. Because she was busy being the Head of the very posh school she is the head of. After that they rang Kiran's mother who is my second emergency number and got her answering machine. So then, in desperation, they rang Daddy in London, and I could hear his voice saying clear as clear, 'Oh God, I am so useless. I should be there. What can I do? What can I do?' and other helpless remarks.

'Oh dear,' they said in the office, and left me on a plastic sofa with a bucket and Molly and Kiran for company, and Kai to apologize. And it was while we were there that Kiran's mother suddenly swirled in, swooped me and the bucket off the sofa, swished Molly and Kiran and Kai down the corridor in front of her (crying 'Go *along*! Go *along*!' as she went) and before we could say a word of protest (not that we thought of it for a moment) we were all four in her car whizzing away as fast as possible under the circumstances i.e. at 30.5 mph.

I don't know what school thought.

That day turned out to be a very good one for several reasons.

1. After five slices of toast and chocolate spread I recovered totally and completely and have never been ill since.
2. Kiran and Molly and I made friends with Kai, and through him the rest of the boys in our class. Which turned out to be very useful (see **Monday 18th December**).
3. Daddy was thoroughly frightened.

70

When I finally reached home today Saffy and Sarah were waiting for me. Sarah had brought me another book.

'I am determined to get you addicted to the things,' she said, handing me a bright pink paperback. 'I cannot bear for you to be missing so much. Try this. It is as unlike poor Gombrich as I could possibly find. Hardly any pictures (and then only black and white and of the crudest kind). Not heavy at all (observe the cheapness of the paper on which it is printed). And utterly relevant to You, Rosy Pose!'

Oh good.

'A family story, you see,' continued Sarah. 'Concerning (I gather, I must admit I only skimmed) a family very like yours. Absent father. Slightly daft mother. No cleaner. Large family of talented children with central focus on the youngest (a remarkable child) . . .'

'Yucky pucky,' I said. 'I think Molly's read that book. I've seen her with something that looks just like it.'

'Very likely,' said Sarah. 'They churn them out by the million. I can get you a never-ending supply if necessary.'

I said she needn't bother. It would almost certainly not be necessary. Then I attempted to change the subject by pretending to sneeze enormously into Kai's fake blood-soaked hanky which he had very kindly lent for the night. It worked superbly. Saffy and Sarah shrieked like witches

71

and hit me. But they didn't forget the book.

'Try it!' ordered Saffron sternly, 'Do not force us to resort to blackmail!' while Sarah begged, 'Oh please read it! Read the first page anyway. Just to get the page-turning habit. It might lead you on to better things.'

After they had gone (Extra Spanish again) I tried to read that book. I really did. Sarah's remarks about the remarkable youngest (to whom I shall refer as R Y) made me slightly curious.

R Y was easy to find, there she was first page, second paragraph, very sorry for herself.

Hmmm.

I hunted her out halfway through and she was still having a bad time.

By the last page R Y was occupying nearly all the print and a quick flick backwards showed that she had been doing this for some chapters. She was getting a lot of attention (lucky old R Y). Was she pleased at this rise to family fame? No. According to her final Big Moan absolutely nothing had improved.

The End

That book has nothing to do with me. Daddy is not absent; he is worrying about me in London. Mummy is not slightly daft; she is sensibly trying to keep her germs in the shed. I suppose Mummy's pictures might really truly be described as daft, if that is all they were. Pictures. But of course, they are not. They are dinner money and bags of apples and car repairs and new trainers and Stayfresh Muffins. And I am NOTHING LIKE that dismal remarkable youngest!

Do you think I will still be moaning on the last page? NO!

Throw the book away!

Tuesday 5th December

David really didn't know what to do with his drum kit last Friday.

And he wasn't busking on Sunday.

Today me and Saffy and Sarah and Indigo all arrived home together and found David on the doorstep, and the drum kit clearly visible through the living-room window.

'I know it's a cheek,' said David, 'but it came on very wet and I had to think of something.'

He had not thought of anything for himself. He must have been outside for ages. He smelled of old damp clothes and his nose was running.

'The rain started just as I got here,' he said, fishing around in his pocket and coming out with a crisp packet and a handful of papier-mâché Economy Peach loo roll. 'And the back door wasn't locked so I put everything inside quick to keep it dry. I've told your mum. She came past while I was sitting round by the front, wondering what to do next. She was rushing for more paint before the shops shut, she said. She was dead nice and she gave me a pound but I don't know how much she took in of what I said.'

Mummy never did quite get the hang of who David actually was. And she always gives money to people who sit around in doorways wondering what to do.

'When it started to rain again I thought it would be all right if I went back in,' continued David. 'But she'd locked up so I didn't like to. Though she's left the key in the door . . .'

So she had: there it was, with its ancient Greenpeace key ring, dangling from the back-door keyhole. What if burglars had come?

'They'd have seen me,' said David.

Yes, I must admit that would probably put most people off. Especially if he had been trying to wipe his nose on a crisp packet like he was doing now.

Anyway, we said he had better come in.

We didn't realize until we got in how much space that drum kit took up. It took up *all* the space. It was an impossible thing to have in the house.

David said he had nowhere else to keep it.

This Is a Short Version of the Story of
Why David Had Nowhere Else to Keep His Drum Kit

David used to keep his drum kit at his grandad's house. David's grandad has always been by far David's best relation. His mum has never liked him much, and neither does his mum's new boyfriend who lives with them. They cannot forget David's awful past when David used to beat up Indigo and shoplift and cause them shame and disgrace with the neighbours. This is a thing that for a long time I couldn't forget either. I used to be very frightened of David. I used to try and make him dead by wishing. I used to hate him. You do hate people who frighten you.

But that's all over now. David has changed.

He still looks the same: big and beached and slightly bemused, like a sea creature that a badly cast spell only just managed to turn into a boy. He still gobbles sweets and gets jokes so slowly you wish you had never spoken. But inside he is completely different.

The opposite of what he was.

There is nothing about David to be afraid of any more.

In fact, we all quite like him.

So we sat him down and listened to what he had to say. About drums.

I've heard David playing drums and it's very loud and monotonous and he never seems to get to the end of a section, or a phrase, or whatever you call a patch of drumming and this is very difficult to bear. Because always, just as the pattern begins to emerge, and the rhythm is finally there, and the big climax is being built and the triumphant crash of the end is in sight . . .

Nothing.

Nothing – like a missing stair.

It's like being jerked flat on your face.

After the nothing there's a hesitating, scratched-together shuffle of bumps and bangs. A go on the cymbals. Heavy breathing over the written-down version of what he's trying to play which he doesn't quite understand.

And then you are dragged all the way back through the beginning again.

Torture.

David's mother could not stand this torture from the first, and so David kept his drum kit at his grandad's and the neighbours said they could feel their windows vibrating but his grandad said, 'You sound champion, boy, and don't let anyone tell you any different.'

It made David warm inside when he heard this, and that was quite often because he practised nearly every day.

But David's mother said, 'He's always spoiled you.'

And, 'If you put half the energy into your school work

that you put into those drums you might make something of yourself. Although I doubt it.'

And, 'It is mixing with that Casson lot that has given you these inflated ideas and what are they anyway? The stories I have heard about those girls would curl your hair, not to mention that mother of theirs who dresses like I shouldn't like to say what. No wonder *he* cleared off.'

She also said, 'When I was your age I was at work. Sixteen. Yes I was. Working.'

And, 'Your grandad is an old man, you know. It's stressful. Stressful for him to have to put up with.'

But worst of all, 'I'll tell you one thing. What with the late hours and the neighbours and the worry you give him with that noise you're going the right way about giving him a heart attack. The right way. Yes.

'And then don't you come crying to me!'

Of course David didn't go crying to her. He came crying to us. Because (this is so unfair I hate to even think the words) David's mother was right. David's very nice grandfather had a heart attack, just as she predicted, fortunately not actually during a drumming recital, but all the same (as his mother didn't hesitate to point out) not long afterwards. And it killed him.

Oh dear.

This story gets worse.

On the awful day when David heard that his grandfather was dead (and that it was probably his fault) and that therefore his mother would now have the enormous job of emptying his grandfather's house of all it contained because the house would be wanted for new people, what did David say?

'Poor Grandad!'? That would have been fine, but he didn't.

'Poor Mum!'? That would have been even better, but he didn't say that either.

No. He cried out, 'Where'll I keep my drum kit? Where'll I keep my drum kit?'

Which was about the worst thing he could have said and proved to his mother that he was all she had long suspected: Heartless, Shameful, Disgraceful and Utterly Selfish.

At this point in the story Saffron and Sarah looked at one another, and their looks said as plainly as if they had spoken, We think David's mother is right.

David didn't see their looks. He went on remembering his grandad.

'He always knew the weather forecast,' he said. 'He liked weather because it came from Abroad. He was very interested in Abroad. He read the labels on things to see where they'd come from and he could always find the places on a map. He liked daft jokes. I used to fetch us both curry while he made tea. When I was little he caught me pinching five pounds from his wallet. "Now, David," he said. "You're saving me a job there. I was going to give you that.'"

David put his face in his hands.

Now Saffron and Sarah looked at each other again, but this time it was a different sort of look.

'Your grandad sounds lovely,' said Sarah. 'Drink your tea.'

David took the mug Indigo handed him and immediately spilled half of its contents on the sofa.

'It doesn't matter,' said Saffron kindly (which is not what she would have said if I had done it) and she did not even flinch when David made it much worse by scrubbing the dampness in with his grimy sweatshirt sleeve.

David looked gratefully from her to Sarah, who were now one on each side of him, patting his back, and he began to perk up. You could see it happening. He unslumped, his tears stopped and he began to look pleased. This is such a weird thing about David that I nearly cannot bear it, the way he can transform from sad to happy so quickly.

I have heard that dogs are the same.

It seems all wrong to me. *I* think David should have been sad about his grandad for about a year, and worried about his drum kit for about six months, and bothered about spilling tea all over the place for at least a couple of days, and *then* he should have started perking up.

After a decent length of dismalness.

However, David, cosily sandwiched between the two most cool and gorgeous and brainy girls in the school, didn't seem to feel the need for dismalness at all.

And of course nobody even hinted that a more sensitive person would no way have revived so unnaturally fast.

We were all very well-behaved indeed.

In the living room, all together.

Around the edge of the drum kit.

The enormous drum kit.

Wednesday 6th December

Today began with Harry Potter and Mr Spencer and it ended with Saffy and the Drum Kit.

Harry Potter and Mr Spencer

'Look what I've brought for you!' said Sarah, coming round before school while I was still eating breakfast (muffins and honey. They need using up). 'I meant to give it to you last night, but I forgot — the drum kit saga drove all lesser matters from my mind. I am sure you'll like Harry Potter. It is the absolute opposite to everything real-life and pink.'

'I know,' I said. 'I've seen the films.'

'This is the adult edition. Sophisticated black cover, you see. Dad bought it to take on holiday . . .'

'Yes, but I *told* you, Sarah. I've seen the films.'

'So no excuses this time! If Dad can read it, anyone can. You know yourself that he's a cultural wasteland (look at his golf picture!). And please stop telling me you've seen the films! I know you have! I watched them with you! Seeing the films has nothing to do with reading the books! Anyway, there isn't time to argue. Where's Saff?'

'She took Mummy up some tea.'

'I'm here now,' said Saffron, appearing as I spoke. 'Are you ready? Can you get the door, Rose? No, forget it! You're covered in honey! Come on, Sarah, let's go!'

With that they whizzed away, rushing for the school bus like it was some new exciting adventure. Saffron and Sarah love school. They've been going for more than twelve years, and the novelty still hasn't worn off. Not like me. I was bored with school by lunchtime on the first day.

But you have to go. It's the law in this country.

So I washed off the honey, said goodbye to Mummy, and left the house. I took Harry Potter with me and Kiran and Molly pounced on him the minute I walked through the playground gates. After that, even though they have both read the book before AND seen the film they spent the rest of the day grabbing it off each other and hunting for their favourite bits to read aloud to anyone who would listen.

'How utterly quaint!' remarked Mr Spencer, creeping up on them, and Molly, not recognizing sarcasm, asked, 'Have you read any of the Harry Potter books, Mr Spencer?'

'I am happy to tell you my life has not yet reached such a level of desperate futility,' replied Mr Spencer.

'Can't believe that,' muttered Kiran, causing Mr Spencer

to exclaim, 'What was that, Kiran? What did you say? Give me that so-called book, please! Give it to me now!'

'It's Rose's,' said Kiran.

'Rose's?' asked Mr Spencer, suddenly very happy. 'Then give it back to Rose, please Kiran! At least in her keeping I can be sure it will remain unread.'

(Oh.

We'll see about *that*, Mr Spencer.)

'He really *isn't* very nice,' remarked Molly, gazing after Mr Spencer as he strutted away, and this made Kiran and I laugh and laugh.

'Well, he *isn't*,' said Molly.

'No,' said Kiran. 'You are quite right, Mollipop! In fact he's so ginormously not very nice that I am surprised he's legal.'

Mr Spencer was in a particularly frightful mood that morning because he had just discovered that although he had successfully cancelled Christmas, he could not get out of the Christmas Class Trip. It's going to happen. Hurray, hurray. On Monday, December 18th. There is a list on the BIG NEWS BOARD (most important noticeboard in the school) of places where we can vote to go. We've got one day to vote. Also (says the BNB) there will be No Hot Lunches served that day, the car park will

84

be closed to make room for the coaches, the school has a wonderful record of good behaviour on these occasions and finally would anyone who has lost items of school uniform in the last few weeks please check out Lost Property which is overflowing with expensive unnamed belongings . . .

'I've done something naughty,' said Molly, as we read all this information to each other at afternoon break (better than going out into the rainy playground).

'What? What?' we asked, but she wouldn't say.

Mr Spencer's rudeness about Harry Potter made me absolutely determined to read it myself. On the way home, I tried.

I tried and I tried, but I couldn't do it. Reading the books after seeing the films felt like going into black and white slow motion with the sound turned off.

Why?

Molly and Kiran can do it.

Perhaps I really am thick.

As soon as I got home I went to see Mummy in the shed to see what she thought. When she understood what I was talking about she explained it straight away.

'It is because you are a very visual person, Rose darling,' she said, holding her chest a bit but looking otherwise fairly well. 'It's all part of the reason that you're so very good at Art. You're so quick at noticing and you have such a good memory that I'm not a bit surprised it's hard to make the transfer from film to book. It's like asking Tom or Indigo to ignore the tune of a song they have heard and just concentrate on the words . . .'

!!!

In our family we have always assumed all the brains came from Daddy. Obviously not quite.

'. . . and if you're comparing yourself with Saffron,' continued my newly-revealed-as-intelligent-mother, '(which you really shouldn't because you and Saffy are very different people) don't forget she could hardly read a word until she was eight. In fact she was quite a lot older than you before she settled down and started working at school . . .'

Yes! Yes! That is true! I had forgotten! Hurray! I knew I wasn't thick.

'And yet look at Saffy now!'

One day I wonder if Mummy will say, 'Look at Rose now!'

'I say it already,' said Mummy, tipping instant coffee

86

into a can of Diet Coke, swirling and swigging. 'And so does Daddy.'

'Who do you say it to?'

'We say it to each other,' said Mummy.

I went back into the house feeling very happy and I had a muffin and some instant hot chocolate to celebrate. Those muffins are *definitely* getting old.

Saffy and the Drum Kit

After my muffin, and before anyone else was home, I went and had a go on David's drum kit. I don't know how he got it all in that wheelbarrow, five drums and three cymbals and stands and pedals too. The cymbals are very crashy, and the drums, especially the big sideways one, are enormously loud. The air shakes when you really wallop them. I can see why David's mother complained. And why his uncomplaining grandad had a heart attack (although maybe he would have had one anyway). (But perhaps not so soon.)

Oh well, he's had it now, and I know it is sad, but at least he has escaped the drums.

Drum kits are not one solid lump: they come apart. They unclip and unscrew. I was very, very tempted to see if I could make David's drum kit any smaller, but I didn't quite dare. I once took a guitar to pieces and the results weren't good. And even if I had got it apart, what then? I don't think that you can let the air out of a drum and fold it flat.

Or can you?

NO, said Indigo and Saffron when they came home at last, but they agreed that the drum kit couldn't stay where it was.

Unless we didn't mind never having a fire or watching TV and could put up with not sitting down ever, unless on the sofa with our knees tucked under our chins.

And we did mind. Very much indeed.

So, after soup and scrambled eggs (Mummy just had soup) we began the Great Drum Kit Removal.

There is not one room in this house where that drum kit will fit. We know because we tried them all.

It could have fitted in the kitchen because our kitchen is big, but we would have had to take out the table and never use the back door, and we would have had to cook very carefully indeed. Saffron and I were sure it could never work, but Indigo said we were just being negative and he went and fetched Mummy out of the shed to see what she thought. Mummy didn't come in, but she peered through the window and said she thought she could manage if the worst came to the worst and she would love a cup of tea with sugar but no milk.

Even making a cup of tea wasn't easy with the drum kit blocking the way to the taps. Sugar was very difficult because it meant opening a cupboard door and that involved pushing everything right up to the cooker and squeezing around. Sarah came to see us while we were in the middle of all this but she had to stay outside until we could open the door. We got her in when we took the tea out and she said (when she had stopped laughing enough to speak), 'What about upstairs on the landing?'

So we tried that next.

It was a dreadful job to get the drum kit up the stairs, and when we finally made it we found the landing had shrunk. The drum kit only fitted there with the bathroom door wide open and the bathroom itself blocked off.

'Fuss, fuss, fuss,' said Sarah. 'I don't see why you can't wash in buckets and go to the loo in the garden. It is only a matter of flexible thinking. You'd better try the bedrooms.'

We started looking in bedrooms.

Mummy's was full of the big bed and about ten million boxes of stuff nobody wants anywhere else.

89

I wouldn't let them try mine. Anyway, it is the smallest room in the house.

Indigo's contains a wardrobe so huge that the door does not open more than halfway, so you have to slide in sideways like a picture on an Egyptian painting.

And then we ended up at the door of the room that Saffy and Caddy used to share.

'Don't even think about it,' said poor Saffy, but of course we did. We had to, there was nowhere else. We piled the beastly drum kit up on Caddy's bed and it sort of fitted.

In an awful kind of way.

'How do you actually feel about it?' Indigo asked Saffron very guiltily indeed.

'I hate it and I am furious,' said Saffron, 'but thank you for asking.'

Thursday 7th December

Communication and Listening

Today's morning assembly was about Communication and Listening. It was really good. It had a Christmas theme.

The Head said, 'Think of the shepherds on the hillside like in the hymn we have just sung. Think of the Wise Men bumping along on their camels through the night. What do you imagine they talked about?'

Classes 1–5 yawned and wriggled. Obviously they didn't want to encourage the Head with any hint of interest. None of them had a single suggestion. They couldn't wait until they were back in their highly decorated classrooms watching School TV. However, we in Class 6 with only Maths and Mr Spencer to look forward to had lots of ideas. We guessed the shepherds probably talked about . . . SHEEP!

'Can we expand on that?' asked the Head hopefully.

Class 6 can expand on anything if it means putting off the evil moment when we have to get down to some work. Kai (especially considering his seat by the bins) is a particularly quick thinker and he immediately asked several intelligent questions which were:

How did the shepherds watch their flocks by night?

Wasn't it dark?

How did they know which flock was which in the dark?

Do sheep go to sleep at night and if not how do they manage to stay awake?

The Head patiently told him (after establishing that he was not trying to be funny) that some sheep go to sleep at night and some do not and that flock-watching was probably a shared occupation so it wouldn't matter which flock was which. (This is not something that I am sure is correct, and the Head himself admitted he was no sheep expert.) He didn't attempt to explain the difficulty of the dark, but hurried us on to the Wise Men bearing gifts.

I was a Wise Man when I was in Class 1, and Mummy made me a costume of such travel-stained sumptuousness that when I put it on the other two Wise Men looked like tramps. So she made them costumes too, and then the shepherds cried and had to be cheered up with carved wooden staffs and plaited sandals and shepherds' pipes that really played. After which the angels and Mary and Joseph looked simply dreary until Mummy organized her Art class of Young Offenders into stringing harps and gilding wings and halos. One Young Offender, who had recently had an unexpected baby, even agreed to lend it for the final scene.

We still have all the things Mummy made at school: every year Class 1 get them out and use them for the Christmas play. Even though they are not as bright as they used to be, and Baby Jesus grew up and we never found another, I still like to see them. My red silk turban is still wonderful with rubies, and the Wise Men are still my favourite characters. They are the only ones in the story who didn't have to be organized by angels.

While I was thinking about all this the others were talking about the subjects the Wise Men would have discussed on their long, long plod to Bethlehem. Kiran nudged me awake when Molly joined in to say (blushing) that she thought they would have talked about Presents. Because, said Molly, when you go to a party you always wonder about the present you are taking, and if it is going to be all right and not exactly the same as someone else is bringing. Or boring.

The Wise Men's presents were definitely not boring. Gold and frankincense and myrrh! I bet Mary didn't even know what they were when she unwrapped them.

'Shops in those days must have been a lot more interesting than shops in these days,' remarked Kiran. 'I can't think of anywhere you could buy gold and frankincense and myrrh any more.'

'Maybe the health food store,' suggested Molly, but the boys thought eBay and the Head said they were probably right.

That assembly on Communication and Listening was the best we ever had and we all (that is Class 6, I mean, Classes 1–5 were nearly dead with boredom) left the hall feeling very communicative and friendly.

A pity Mr Spencer missed it.

Mr Spencer spent the time we were away rearranging our classroom.

Now all our tables are separated, and not one person sits with a friend. In fact, it looks to me that we have been deliberately placed with our enemies. Kiran is with Ravi who is going to be a surgeon and reads books about the insides of people and cannot wait to start slicing us up. Molly, who has no enemies, has been given a table on her own at the back. And other sufferers are similarly arranged. Only I am lucky. I am with Kai, probably because Mr Spencer remembered how we fought in PE. But ha, ha, Mr Spencer, we have since become good friends! Kai and I have agreed to conceal this though, and every time Mr Spencer glances our way we take care to look sullen, and now and then we give each other nasty hard shoves. (This causes happy twitches to Mr Spencer's moustache but no other reaction.)

For the whole morning our classroom was very quiet. Not surprising: nobody had anyone to talk to. At lunchtime things became a little better. It was too wet to go outside, and we stayed in the classroom and talked. The class Christmas trip had to be decided upon that day.

This was our list of choices:

1. The pantomime (Dick Whittington).
2. The Ice Rink.
3. London, to look in the Science Museum and the Natural History Museum and the V & A afterwards if there is time.
4. The Zoo.

'The Zoo, the Zoo, the Zoo! *Please* the Zoo!' begged Molly.
Groan.

I have been dragged round that zoo at least a thousand times. It is only a few miles away. When Caddy lived here it was her favourite place, her home-from-home. She knew all the staff and all the animals. When she was little she got a season ticket for Christmas every year, but by the time she finished school she did not need tickets any more. They let her in like they did the postman. Later, when she was a student she had holiday jobs there. (Hence Molly's laminated autograph.)

Of all the places I would not like to visit at Christmas the Zoo is the one I would not like to go to most. It is utterly dreary in wintertime, miles and miles of damp gritty paths, and all the animals asleep or invisible.

I made a speech to Class 6 explaining this. 'Vote for London!' I urged.

'If I have to go all the way to London on a coach I will be sick,' said Molly. 'I always am. Travel sickness tablets don't work on me.'

'Nor me,' agreed several people.

'All the Christmas lights will be on!' I said. 'And nobody need worry about being sick. Mr Spencer will take a bucket. The teachers always do.'

Mr Spencer overheard this remark, and looked so utterly revolted that I could see if we got to London it would be over his dead body. So I changed my tactics and started pleading for the pantomime instead.

Kiran wanted the pantomime too. That was her first choice. She had a cousin who had already been with *her* school and she had told Kiran all about it. Sweets had been hurled by the bucketful down from the stage to the audience and a new and very rude version of 'Rudolph the Red-Nosed Reindeer' had been learned. Best of all, two rats and the Cat had personally invaded the audience and hauled the teachers on stage to help bake a very messy wedding cake.

'They used real eggs and flour and shaving foam,' said Kiran, 'and all the teachers got covered but it didn't matter because they'd made them put on coloured wellies and rain hats.

I should have loved to see Mr Spencer on stage in coloured wellies and a rain hat, but somehow I couldn't imagine it happening. Nor could I see him on skates, even though the Ice Rink was the first choice of nearly all the boys. As Mr Spencer listened to our discussions his face had become more and more unreadable, set like concrete into a bland empty smile. Kai told a story about melting ice and fractured skulls and he did not even flinch.

I thought, *Mr Spencer has decided*.

It is not going to be London; no way will he deal with that bucket. And it is not going to be the pantomime either. Might it be the Ice Rink? Might he have a secret talent for skating without fracturing his skull or losing his dignity in a puddle?

Maybe.

But.

I have a very gloomy feeling that it will be the Zoo.

We voted at break this afternoon and Mr Spencer counted up the votes and announced the result himself and then he hurried away (with all the voting papers) to book the coach and the tickets before we could argue.

It is the Zoo.

We have been swizzed! Mr Spencer has rigged the vote so that he doesn't have to go up on stage or skate or supervise the sick bucket all the way to London and back.

Boo. Hiss. Throw him to the lions.

However, Molly is very pleased, and on the way home she told me and Kiran the very naughty thing that she did.

Molly put the Zoo on the list!

There were three things originally; Molly added a fourth.

Molly!

'But *how?*' demanded Kiran and I. 'And *why?*'

'I saw the list on Mr Spencer's desk and borrowed his pen and wrote it on the bottom,' said Molly, 'because I have wanted . . . I've always wanted . . . Do you remember on Saturday when you promised you would help me with that thing I have always wanted to do?'

'Yes,' we said (suspiciously).

'Good,' said Molly.

'But you never said what it actually was.'

'Just something,' said Molly, skipping off towards her house. 'Don't worry! It won't be boring! I have got it nearly all worked out. Biscuits. Torches. Space blankets . . . See you tomorrow!'

'*Space blankets!*' repeated Kiran and me to each other, and I said, 'Kiran, do you think Molly *really* has thought of something?'

'No,' said Kiran. 'Not Molly.'

'She thought of the Zoo.'

'Hmm,' said Kiran, and then after a while she added, 'So she did.'

Friday 8th December

Mothers

Today Mummy (nagged into it by Saffy and Indigo) went to the doctors'. They gave her some antibiotics which they told her should make her feel slightly better in two days, and completely better in seven. 'So, superb,' she croaked, waving the bottle at us. 'Nothing to worry about for a week and I went shopping on the way home.'

Shopping was more muffins and more apples and lots of frozen pizza and boxes of herbal teas but I was most interested in the antibiotics because I had thought Mummy was nearly better.

I followed her to the shed to check this out.

'Of course I'm better,' promised Mummy. 'I have a slight secondary infection which the doctor told me is so common it is hardly worth treating. In fact he has a big notice on his door saying DO NOT COME IN IF YOU HAVE ANY OF THESE SYMPTOMS and then a list of everything I've got.'

'Then why did you go in?' I asked.

'I was trapped,' explained Mummy. 'Because I had made an appointment and they have another notice up saying MISSED APPOINTMENTS ARE NOT JUST EXPENSIVE BUT BAD MANNERS and then a list of all the trouble that missed appointments cause. So I went in. The Expensive Bad Manners poster was bigger than the Do Not Come In one, so it won. I am afraid I am out of my element at the doctors'. I find the whole experience totally confusing, starting with the car park where you are not allowed to park . . .'

She was trying very hard to make me laugh, and so I did. This perked her up tremendously and she began reading the instructions on her antibiotics.

'No alcohol,' she remarked. 'That will be interesting. I've stockpiled on herbal teas to compensate. I'll make some straight away. What are you looking at, Rose darling?'

I was looking at the pictures scattered all over the table, a dozen versions of St Matthew's and its tombstones slipping and sliding across unnatural-looking skies.

'Just roughs,' said Mummy, spraying tea tree oil around and coughing. 'Horrible old St Matthew's, it is so not me. At college I was happiest with nudes but whether there's a local demand is a very moot point. . .'

We both looked towards the window, black rain

splattering against black glass, the bare branches of the fig tree outlined like long bony arms against the light from the kitchen.

'Not *obvious* nude territory . . .' said Mummy, and this time I couldn't help laughing for real.

'. . . but perhaps in spring I will give it a trial! Off you go now, Rosy Pose. Back to the house and keep cosy. I'll pop across and see you at bedtime.'

She was sounding much better, and sipping her herbal tea (fennel and honey) as if she really liked it. So I went. But I looked back towards the window when I got to the house. Mummy was drooping over her table with the fennel and honey mug pressed against her chest. When she saw me looking she waved her antibiotics and smiled.

I was glad she was coming to see me at bedtime.

Quite late in the evening David turned up. Indigo was out and Saffron was upstairs doing her homework so I got stuck with him. I gave him the job of finishing up the getting-old muffins and he did it very quickly without even the aid of chocolate spread. There was something a bit odd about David that night. First he said he had come to see if his drum kit was all right, and then that he had a little favour to ask Indigo, and then he said it didn't matter. He was very jumpy and he kept wandering about, peering behind things until at last it dawned on me that he was looking for his drums. I thought that was very funny and I let him carry on hunting until Saffy came down and told him that they were stuck in her bedroom and the sooner he took them away the better. It seemed to surprise David that we had not wanted to keep them in our living room, but he didn't complain, except to say, 'I shan't be able to practise, then?'

'No!' said Saffy, very firmly indeed.

Not long after that Saffron answered a very odd telephone call. It was from David's mother.

'Have you got David there?' she asked in a very unfriendly way (Saffron told us).

'Yes,' said Saffron. 'He has been here for some time. And so has his drum kit.'

'Ho,' said David's mother, 'I knew it!' and was gone.

David was very pleased indeed when he heard about this phone call. He said, 'That'll put her off.'

Mummy didn't come in for ages and ages after I went to bed, but at last I heard her on the stairs. She opened my door very quietly and whispered, 'Sweet dreams, darling.'

Then I let myself go to sleep.

Twelve Shopping Days Until Christmas

I woke up this morning with a panicky feeling that it was much later than usual. I was out of bed and hunting for socks before I remembered that it was the weekend at last.

Snores were coming from Indigo's room (very unusual for a Saturday) and coughs from Mummy's, but Saffy's door was wide open and her room was scattered with the sort of stuff people leave around when they are rushing away to brighter places. Open books, a smell of perfume, styling tongs still warm.

I often wonder what it must be like to be Saffron. I will never know, Saffy says, because I am useless at multi-tasking. Kiran agrees that this is true, but she says it does not matter, she is good enough for both of us. Kiran is good at everything except Art, but (hurray!) *I* am good enough for both of us at that. So we make a great team, and when we are grown-up we plan to live together and I will earn a lot of money and Kiran will do all the work. She is going to be my very expensive secretary.

I like to have a chat with my secretary (at present she doesn't charge) on Saturday mornings, but when I telephoned her home there was no one in. Instead I got a new answerphone message, recorded by Kiran.

'We are sorry we cannot take your call right now. Everyone has gone Christmas shopping. (By the way did you know there are only twelve shopping days left till Christmas?) If you would like to leave a message please keep it short and ROSE do not start speaking until after the tone.'

The message I left must have sounded like a howl. Twelve shopping days left till Christmas! I don't think my family realize that. I am sure no one in this house has done any Christmas shopping except me.

I think I should warn them how close we are to disaster.

I do this by going very quietly downstairs and writing *TWELVE SHOPPING DAYS TILL CHRISTMAS* in magic marker pen on the face of the kitchen clock.

That made me feel very much better and after I had done it I went back up to my bedroom to gloat over my own Christmas shopping which I bought ages ago in September the day after I got my birthday money.

Here is a List of My Christmas Shopping
KIRAN: Invisible ink pen to write me secret messages.

MOLLY: Cat and rabbit shaped cookie cutters.

SARAH: Pirate bandana.

SAFFY: Book called *1001 Jokes for Intellectuals*.

MUMMY: A lovely mug that says WORLD'S BEST EVER MOTHER.

DADDY: Another lovely mug that says WORLD'S BEST EVER DAD because I don't want him to be upset if he sees Mummy's.

MICHAEL: A key ring like a tiny snowstorm with a place to put in a photo (I put in Caddy).

CADDY: Another key ring, just the same only with Michael's photograph.

TOM MY BRILLIANT GUITAR-PLAYING FRIEND IN AMERICA: (I do not have this present to gloat over any more because I posted it two weeks ago. Maybe it is in New York right now, where it will be only five in the morning and he will still be asleep).

I bought Tom a new strap for his guitar. Indigo came with me to help choose. It was very hard to pick the best; there were loads of good ones, there was even one with roses on. I looked and looked, and at last I chose the most expensive of all. It was woven to look like gorgeous red and yellow flames.

'He'd like the roses even better,' said Indigo, grinning at me. 'Go on, Rosy Pose!'

I had wanted to buy the rose one right from the beginning.

'Look what he sent you for your birthday!' urged Indigo.

He sent a tiny silver guitar, threaded on to a guitar string instead of a chain. (When I lost it two weeks later and cried he sent another.)

So I bought the rose strap, and later I went back and got the flame one for Indigo. I had just enough money, although it wouldn't have mattered if I hadn't because I could have got him a mug saying WORLD'S BEST EVER BROTHER.

Which would have been true.

But

I have two worries:

1. How can I give Caddy her present if I don't know where she is?

2. Should I really give Michael a present at all? Last year I didn't, and then felt awful because he sent one to me, a lovely silky bag, all the way from Italy. But this last year, since he came home, I have not spoken to him once. When he drives past in his driving instructor car he never sees my waves and he must have found a new place to live – the birthday card I sent came back with a note on the envelope saying ADDRESS NOT KNOWN.

Michael has become a mystery. Did Caddy find him when she disappeared after her non-wedding day with all the postcards he had ever sent me? She intended to, and I think she must have, there came a time when she stopped mentioning him in her telephone calls.

Perhaps it was a sad finding.

A long time ago Michael and I went shopping together. We bought a diamond and platinum engagement ring for Caddy. I have it now. Michael asked me to look after it until he and Caddy needed it again.

I've looked after it for a long time.

I would like to give it back.

Pause.

My pause ended with hunger and I went back to the kitchen to hunt for food, and while I was there I had the very good idea of taking Mummy breakfast in bed. Microwave porridge and orange juice. I made enough for both of us.

'Goodness!' said Mummy when she saw it. 'What a treat! I don't know when I last had breakfast in bed. Porridge! My favourite!'

'Eat it then,' I said, and she did, every bit. I watched her.

I had my breakfast sitting on the end of her bed to keep her company. This bothered Mummy because she thought I would breathe in germs. To stop her worrying I opened the bedroom window as far as it would go and breathed fresh air from that direction. It was very fresh indeed, gusty and wild-smelling and scattered with snowflakes. It flung the curtains into loops and scattered clothes on the floor and rocked the pots and vases on the windowsill and I felt as if I'd let a winter poltergeist into the house.

'Isn't it exciting?' I said.

'It's like having breakfast on the roof!' agreed Mummy, huddling her dressing gown around her, 'or the deck of a ship, or the side of a mountain! What are you going to do with yourself this morning, Rosy Pose?'

'Probably wrap up my Christmas presents again.' (I have wrapped them several times already but I can never resist the temptation to have One Last Look.)

'Thank goodness I don't have to bother with All That,' said Mummy in a most unChristmassy way. 'But I must get those pictures of St Matthew's finished somehow. I'd better stop wallowing in comfort, get back to my solitary cell . . .'

'You said it was a stony tower before,' I reminded her.

'Stony tower, cell or dungeon, it's all the same,' said Mummy, getting out of bed and staggering as the wind hit her. 'One of those places where you need a knight in shining armour to come galloping by . . .'

Then she wobbled off towards the bathroom, holding

on to doors and walls and things like she really was on the deck of a ship, and I wrestled the window closed and took the plates downstairs. There (bad surprise, bad surprise) I found David, furtively reading the porridge box.

I didn't ask David to explain himself, but he seemed to feel he should.

David was at our house all night, asleep on Indigo's ancient Jungle Book bedside rug.

(Those were the snores I had heard!)

Indigo went out to his Saturday job ages ago. He knows David stayed over. I think.

(I'm sure he does. It would be pretty hard not to notice something the size of David making a loud noise on the floor.)

Anyway, this is what David told me:

He says he's left his home for ever. It is not as if he ever liked it.

(Oh dear.)

He hasn't been back for days. Friends have allowed him to sleep on bits of floor, Josh and Marcus and Patrick and now us.

(I hope this story is going to have a happy ending?)

David's mother's last words to her son were 'Go and see if your so-called-artistic-hippy-friends will take you in!'

(Meaning us!)

And, thanks to Saffy's remarks on the phone last night she probably thinks he has been here all the time. Not that she will be bothered, says David. She is not like our mum, and if she was he wouldn't have had to get away. Also his mum's boyfriend will be dead chuffed he is out of the house at last and school will never know a thing about it, as long as he keeps turning up and causes no trouble.

(Oh David.)

Today he is going to sort out a really good place where he can settle down for a bit.

Here?

Not here.

Phew!

But he wouldn't mind some porridge, if that would be all right.

Of course it is all right! Almost anything is all right, so long as he doesn't move in!

'As soon as I am dressed I will make you as much porridge as you like,' I told David. 'I can do hot chocolate too, if you want.'

'Oh no, oh no,' said David, sounding very shocked. 'I didn't mean you had to get it, Rose!'

David can cook!

He made porridge for himself, and then he made lovely omelettes with bits of tomato in for both of us, and afterwards a special chocolate milkshake for me. And to finish this truly spectacular performance he washed all the messy plates, wiped the surfaces free of crumbs, emptied the bin, scrubbed out the sink, swept the floor, and put everything away.

Good grief!

In the living room he plumped the cushions, lined up the books in the bookcase, threw out the chrysanthemums that had been smelling weird for days, tidied the hearth, lit the fire and carried in extra coal from the place where we keep it outside the back door.

'There then,' said David, fetched a big greasy backpack down from Indigo's room, and went.

Sunday 10th December

Some of the News is Very Good

Caddy telephoned again today. That's the second time in two weeks after hardly a word for months.

'It was so lovely to speak to you last Saturday,' she said. 'You really cheered me up . . .'

Did you need cheering up then, Caddy?

'. . . and it was brilliant to be able to ring home without being bombarded by ten million silly questions . . .'

Yes. OK. I can take that big hint.

'Your awful teacher, Rose. I've been thinking about him all week. Has he really cancelled Christmas?'

Imagine Caddy worrying about Mr Spencer all week! How ridiculous. If she'd had a week like I've just had (Mummy in a dungeon, fainted in school, 'Cheer up Rose there are children starving in Africa' – I must do something about that next – not to mention ninety-six muffins in various stages of decomposition . . .)

If Caddy had had a week like mine, Mr Spencer would have been the last thing on her mind!

But I didn't say that, because I was so pleased to be talking to her again, and despite her stress-free week, she had obviously telephoned for a second dose of unquestioning cheerfulness. Also I didn't want her disappearing back into the Faraway-Natural-History-Related-Uncommunicative-Fog from which she had so recently begun to emerge. So I skipped all questions I would like to have asked her, resisted the temptation to describe my week of disasters and started on: The News!

I told her selected items of my Christmas shopping, and about the cupboards being so full of food we can hardly close the doors and all the different ways we had got the better of Mr Spencer at school in the last few days.

'Good! Good!' exclaimed Caddy.

I told her that Tom had emailed from New York saying 'Guess what I chose for Christmas!' and how I kept emailing back guesses but all he said was 'Try again'.

'It will be a guitar,' said Caddy. 'Obviously!'

'He's got one.'

'Yes, but you know guitar players,' said Caddy. 'They never have enough guitars. They always want another. Anything else?'

'Like what?'

'More good news?' said Caddy greedily.

As a matter of fact, I did have more good news, but I was not at all sure what it would do to Caddy. However, I told her anyway.

'A Christmas card from Michael,' I said, and paused for her reply. When it didn't come I carried on, 'He's back home, you know. Teaching people to drive again. I quite often see his car.'

Still no comment from Caddy.

'Well, anyway, inside the card it says *Season's Greetings, Meilleurs Voeux, Felices Fiestas, Frohe Festtage* and something in Greek (Saffy said) and something else in Chinese. It's one of those sorts of cards.'

'Oh.'

'And Michael has written . . .'

'What? What?' demanded Caddy, like she was waking up from sleep. 'What has he written?'

'. . . *"Today I saw 5 dressed up Santas, 4 snowflakes, 3 girls who looked a bit like Caddy, 2 many Christmas trees to count, 1 football match, no Roses although it would have been nice, love Michael."*

'Three girls who looked a bit like me?' repeated Caddy. 'Three? Three! Oh! Oh! Oh!'

(One 'Oh' for each girl.)

'I thought you'd be pleased,' I told her. 'I was.'

In fact, when I found Michael's card on the mat this morning (hand-delivered, no stamp) and saw what was written inside, I had been completely overwhelmed.

'Why should I be pleased that he saw three girls who looked like me?' asked Caddy, as if she really wanted to know.

'It means he thought of you at least three times in one day. Isn't that good?'

'Is it?' said Caddy, very doubtfully.

Caddy never used to be doubtful about Michael. She fell in love with him the first time she saw him (and so did we all, and not surprising, Michael is one of the nicest people in the world).

Caddy didn't hide her feelings for Michael. (In those days Caddy never hid anything from anyone.) She pursued him with relentless adoration until he gave in and fell in love with her too. Which he did very strongly indeed. Too strongly for Caddy: she dumped him. Michael went away, travelling with a friend called Luke. So that was the end of Caddy and Michael, except sometimes he sent postcards back to me.

Then Caddy decided to marry someone else instead.

The someone was called Alex and he was a slightly famous

wildlife photographer which was very nice for Caddy, I suppose, because she had someone to talk to about animals at last. So then we all had to get to know Alex and put up with him prancing about with light meters and talking very importantly to very important people on his mobile phone, saying, 'Yes, yes! Right. Oh no! Absolutely! Fly it past! Cool!'

That's who Caddy was going to marry, only she was saved at the last moment by a chance remark.

Of mine.

In church.

At the altar.

Halfway through the wedding service. And I am never ever going to another wedding again as long as I live.

Not that anyone would invite me, I don't suppose.

After last time.

Well, so instead of marrying Alex and whizzing off on her honeymoon, Caddy came to her senses and realized how terrifyingly close she had come to marrying the wrong man. And where was the right one?

Somewhere in Europe on a motorbike, trying to forget her.

Caddy did the only sensible thing she could do. She nicked all my postcards from Michael and set off to hunt for him. And that wasn't such a daft idea as it sounds, because Michael and Luke were not travelling fast, they were picking up odd jobs in different places and repairing their bikes and making friends. Michael's messages told all this in black Biro jokey sentences on the backs of pictures of donkeys in rose-trimmed hats, and villas with roses on the walls and blue seas and city roofs with hand-drawn roses raining from the sky . . .

I bet I could have found Michael easily.

But Caddy couldn't.

For the first few months she telephoned from time to time to tell us how she was getting on, and to hear the news from home and to describe her latest weird zoological job (Parrot Rescue, Coypu Monitoring, Spanish Birdwatching Tours, Australian Rabbit Counting, No, that last one isn't true. I made it up), but all the time it felt like she was drifting further and further away.

And then we lost track of her.

Until now.

What is she doing?

I wish she would come back home.

'I wish you would come back home,' I said.

'I am home.'

'I mean really here.'

'Oh Rosy Pose,' said Caddy. 'I don't know if you would wish that if I was really there.'

And then she was gone.

Monday 11th December

The Trouble With Molly

Kiran called for me on the way to school this morning and reminded me that it was dinner-money day. In our family dinner money comes from the housekeeping jar on the kitchen mantelpiece. It is stuffed with as much money as we can lay our hands on, we all help ourselves to whatever is needed, and it isn't counted.

When Kiran first heard of this arrangement she was outraged.

'But what is to stop you taking as much as you like?' she demanded. 'And buying anything you wanted? You could!'

Well, I suppose I could. Like I could leave the taps running in the bathroom upstairs and bring down the kitchen ceiling. Or I could eat every single biscuit in the biscuit tin and then set the house on fire.

'Just because I could,' I told Kiran, 'doesn't mean I will!'

But she was not convinced.

'Are you telling me,' she demanded, 'that nothing has ever gone wrong with the housekeeping jar?'

Long ago Caddy and Saffron spent the entire contents on a party dress for me and we had to eat quite a lot of plain pasta before it was filled up again. Once, at the same time as one of Caddy's boyfriends was visiting, all the notes mysteriously disappeared. Sometimes it is just plain empty, and occasionally it's lost (Caddy used to take the whole jar with her shopping).

But, nearly always, the jar is on the mantelpiece and there is something in it, and Kiran has got used to us now, and no longer stares when I fish for my dinner money. She is also accustomed to how a hamster family lives wild in the walls, and the way Indigo plays guitar with Sarah on his knee, and Mummy lives in the shed, and Daddy appears and disappears like the moon between clouds on a stormy night, and Saffron is my sister as well as my cousin. And even to how nobody minded when Caddy changed her mind about who she wanted to marry on her actual wedding day.

Which just shows that you can get used to almost anything.

'Why does it say *TWELVE SHOPPING DAYS TILL CHRISTMAS* on your clock?' asked Kiran, poking round the kitchen while I finished packing my school bag.

'I just thought everyone ought to know.'

'But it isn't!'

'It was on Saturday when I wrote it.'

'You need to change it.'

'It won't come off.'

'Oh, Rose!' said Kiran. 'Show me what pen you used!'

So I showed her and she added to my message on the clock. Now it says:

On Saturday 9th December there were
TWELVE SHOPPING DAYS TILL CHRISTMAS
(not counting Sundays)

I was not pleased when I saw this. It does not look scary at all any more. It just looks like a chatty remark. And now there is so much writing on the clock you can hardly see the numbers.

Bother.

Outside the school gates the cheerful face of the lollipop lady reminded me of another of my problems.

'Did you know that there are children starving in Africa?' I asked Kiran.

'Everyone knows. Of course I knew,' said Kiran, but she didn't offer any solution.

I hope this is not another thing that Kiran has managed to get used to.

Just inside the entrance hall of our school there is a

plastic collecting box labelled OXFAM. We all walk past it every day.

Sometimes you can get used to too much.

There is one good thing that Mr Spencer has achieved by mixing up where we sit and being impartially nasty to all of us together: he has made us all friends. Today, when it was Class 6's turn to take their dinner money to the office a very nice thing happened.

We have to line up to pay in alphabetical order which means that I am always first in the queue because nobody happens to have a second name beginning with A or B. C is the first. That is me. Rose Casson.

'Dinner money, Rose?' says Mrs Shah, our very nice school secretary.

'I am not having dinners this week,' I tell her.

'Oh,' says Mrs Shah, very surprised because I have had dinners every day since I was five. 'I am sorry to hear that because it is Christmas Lunch on Thursday and two hundred crackers are languishing in my office even as we speak. I trust our Culinary Department has not disappointed you in any way? I believe they are aspiring to Home-made Cheesy Mash today.'

'They have not disappointed me at all,' I say as politely

123

as I can because Saffron and Sarah have often advised me that in a formal situation it is advantageous to reply in a style similar to that with which one is addressed. 'Not at all. Not even with the broccoli (you cannot be disappointed if you know what to expect) and Cheesy Mash is one of my favourites. The reason I am not having dinners is that I have put all my dinner money in the Oxfam box in the hall because there are children starving in Africa which doesn't cheer me up.'

'Nor me, Rose,' said Mrs Shah, looking at me very kindly. 'Go to the back of the queue, dear, while I have a little think.'

But she did not need her little think after all, because by the time I was in front of her desk again I had my dinner money and quite a lot over, passed back down the queue to me by my friends in Class 6, none of whom were cheered up by the thought of children starving in Africa either.

'Very well done!' said Mrs Shah, as I stuffed the excess in the Oxfam box. 'Tell your friends that I congratulate them all! It is amazing what you people can accomplish when you work as a team and although I must admit that broccoli is on the menu again you might like to spread the word that it's Chocolate Tarmac for pudding with pink milkshake.'

So I went back to class and did this, and they were all very pleased, especially Molly. And yet Molly had no spare dinner money to give me (Molly's mother being the sort of person who puts the exact amount in a labelled envelope). And Molly doesn't like Tarmac, or milk in any form, not even pink.

'Why are you so happy?' I asked her, making an excuse to pass her lonely table at the back of the room. 'Is it still about the Zoo?' And she nodded and nodded, all rosy and smiling to herself.

The trouble with Molly is that she watches too much educational TV. She has about ten million David Attenborough DVDs too. She thinks he is marvellous. She has a great big picture of him patronizing a gorilla on her bedroom wall.

It was on this day that Kiran and I first heard what we had promised to help Molly to do.

Kiran was very very unhappy when she found out. I didn't mind so much for two reasons:

1. I (sort of) understood. I was brought up with wild hamsters, don't forget, and too many guinea pigs, and Caddy.

2. I really didn't believe it could happen, no matter *how* much Mrs Shah believed Class 6 could accomplish when they worked together as a team.

Tuesday 12th December

Anything for a Bit of Peace

At two o'clock this morning Saffy and Indigo and I went downstairs to see if the strange noises and freezing draughts that had woken us were caused by ghosts or merely burglars.

We discovered Mummy instead, gobbling aspirin. 'The thing about antibiotics,' said Mummy, 'is that they quite often make you much worse before they make you better. It just proves they are working. Go to bed, darlings, I'm quite all right.'

'You look terrible,' said Saffy sternly.

'I always look terrible at two o'clock in the morning,' Mummy replied, splashing cold tap water on her face. 'Please don't close the window, Indy, fresh air kills germs.'

'Hypothermia,' said Indigo, not obeying, 'kills people. And anyway, Rose's lips are going blue.'

'Rose, go to bed!' ordered everyone.

I thought this would be a good time to start being stubborn so I said that I wouldn't go to bed unless Mummy went too. Mummy protested a bit because she said lying down made her cough and the sound of her coughing would keep us awake.

'Not as much as the idea of you down here alone and freezing to death will keep us awake,' pointed out Saffy.

By then I had got my teeth to chatter in a quite realistic way, so Mummy gave in and staggered back upstairs and I went after her. I was nearly as cold as I was pretending to be, and I thought I wouldn't get to sleep for ages, but Indigo made me a hot-water bottle and Saffy gave me a new book from Sarah, and after ten minutes in bed with these things nothing in the world could keep me awake.

The book was called *Where the Wild Things Are*. It was very short, but it got into my dreams. In the book a boy's bedroom walls melt away and a forest grows. The illustrations of this happening were brilliant. In my dreams the same thing happened to me, and my dream forest was so beautiful and so vivid that as soon as I woke up I took all the pictures and posters and clocks and postcards off my bedroom walls and started to draw it before it faded from my mind. There was only time to sketch in the outlines before I went to school, but all day in spare moments I planned my forest.

This drove Kiran mad.

'Please pay attention *sometimes*, Rose!' she ordered, when I kept losing track of the day-long argument that was happening between her and Molly. 'You're not listening to anything and just saying, "Yes, yes, yes" to shut us up. Admit it!'

'Yes.'

'Well don't, because it makes it sound like you agree with every single thing Molly says!'

'I thought she really did agree with everything I said,' said Molly reproachfully. 'Don't you, Rose?'

'Yes,' I said (anything for a bit of peace). 'Of course I do!'

The forest I drew in my bedroom was a fir wood. I drew it with chalk and charcoal: ordinary, smudgy, coloured chalks, and silvery charcoal. The trees were Christmas trees, grey-green snow-laden branches reaching to the sky. Among the branches I put a crescent moon and dim glowing stars of peach and blue and yellow and purple scattered very rarely, lighting the snow.

The thing about drawing is knowing when to stop. I finished my fir wood all in one evening and then I let everyone come and look.

'Wonderful, lovely, perfect,' croaked Mummy.

'Hurray!' exclaimed Sarah triumphantly. 'I know where

129

you got that idea from. At last I found a book you like!'

'I thought you'd grown out of drawing on walls,' said Saffron. 'Bill will go mad!' (Daddy is Bill.) 'He's only just paid up to have the last lot obliterated.' (She was talking about the kitchen and the stairs, recently repainted Scrubbable Magnolia and now officially declared an Art-Free Zone.)

'I don't see why she can't draw what she likes on her own bedroom walls,' said Indigo. 'It looks amazing, doesn't it, David?'

'It's really good,' said David who was round at our house *again*. 'If it's finished. Anyway, I expect it will paint over. Me and Grandad emulsioned his upstairs once and covered over worse marks than that.'

Indigo gripped David by the elbow and put him next to the door so he would have somewhere to run if I threw anything and said to distract me, 'There was a mysterious phone call for you earlier, Rose. Someone called Molly said to tell you only five nights to wait and then she rang off.'

'Five nights till what?' I asked (distracted).

'She didn't say. I was going to ask you.'

How strange. I don't remember agreeing to anything. What had she and Kiran been arguing about today? I don't know. Perhaps I should (as Kiran commanded) start paying attention sometimes.

So I did.

Saffy and Sarah and Mummy had all disappeared. Indigo was saying to David, 'I'm just going out. Do you want to come too or are you going to stay here and risk Death by Charcoal with Rose?'

'I'll stay with Rose,' I heard David say as they went downstairs. 'I only came to ask if I could borrow your washing machine . . .'

What!

David must be mad. Of course he can't borrow our washing machine. We've only got one and we need it ourselves. We use it nearly every day. Just because he has dumped his drum kit on us doesn't mean he can go off with our washing machine in exchange.

I fumed for a few minutes and then went downstairs to defend our property. There was David, alone in the kitchen, watching his socks and things go round and round.

Oh.

That sort of borrow.

Well, that is OK. I thought he planned to take it away, on his wheelbarrow, like the drum kit.

But why can't David wash his clothes in his mother's washing machine at home?

131

Because (says David) he is still not living at his mum's.

Nor at Marcus's.

Or Patrick's.

Or Josh's.

Where then?

David is living in his dead grandad's attic. Which is a Big Secret that I must never ever let on to anyone (however I've made no promises).

Anyway, David has been Up There since Saturday.

And it is Great.

David's dead grandad's house is cleared out and empty, waiting for the next tenants, but David still has the back door key that his grandad gave him years and years ago. And although the electricity is off, the water is still running, and that is the main thing.

Is it?

Yes, said David, slightly embarrassed, because then you can flush the loo.

I suppose.

And wash.

Oh good.

And cook.

Can you?

Soup and stuff. On a camp stove which is also up in the attic (only accessible by the attic trapdoor stairs which David pulls up and folds away every night). Also in the attic are David's backpack, now unpacked, his sleeping bag and school books.

School books?

David is keeping up at school with homework and stuff, so nobody notices anything is wrong. In fact, he is working harder than he has ever done in his life before and the teachers are dead impressed. Besides, it passes the time without a telly. It is dark in the attic although there is a skylight, but David does his homework by candlelight. (The candlelight doesn't show from outside, he has checked.)

I think candles in attics in empty houses sound dangerous.

No, they're not, says David. Not if you are very careful. It is brilliant up in the attic; it's like a camp.

It sounds awful.

Not at all. You can even, in the attic, practise the drums a bit on empty cardboard boxes.

David would stay there for ever if he could.

This cannot happen. One day someone else will come and live in David's dead grandad's house and then what? They are bound to notice a great big teenage boy playing drums

133

and cooking soup in the attic.

'Well,' said David, when I pointed this out. 'You can't worry about everything.'

I thought myself that David wasn't worrying about *anything*, but he explained that he was taking one day at a time, hoping his Post Office money would hold out until January when he would be sixteen and could get a Saturday job in the supermarket stacking shelves.

David told me all this quite calmly, while his washing went round and round, first in the washer and then in the dryer, and I didn't go away because I'd had a thought.

Now that David's grandad is dead, nobody in the whole world except Indigo cares very much about David.

And if I have worries (like Mr Spencer and what Molly is talking about and where is Caddy and how ill is Mummy and what kind of a Christmas is this going to be if nobody does anything about it, not to mention always wondering what time it is in New York), then David has worse ones.

I didn't like to go back upstairs and leave him alone, and so I kept him company and after a while I offered to make toast for supper. I had missed the earlier version of this meal that Saffy had produced because I was not hungry at the time. But now my forest was finished that feeling was past and I was suddenly starving.

'Starving?' asked David.

Then with no further fuss he made delicious Welsh rarebit for me and him, and a poached egg and a cup of weak tea for Mummy which he took out to her stony tower, dismal dungeon, black hole, shed.

'It's funny,' he said when he came back (glowing because Mummy had been very pleased with the tea and polite about the egg), 'a lot of people would think it was weird, the way your mum hangs out in that shed—'

'It is not weird at all,' I interrupted defensively. 'She is just staying there because of her painting and germs. It makes perfect sense.'

'I know,' said David, 'that's what I was going to say. Just like it makes perfect sense for me to live in the attic.'

He sounded very pleased indeed when he said this, like he had proved something that really mattered.

So I didn't argue.

But I did wonder.

'What would your mum do if she found out?' I asked.

'Kill me,' said David.

Oh.

She'd better not find out then.

Wednesday 13th December

Only at Night

Today at lunchtime Molly told Kai and Kiran and me that David Attenborough says only at night can you truly feel the magnificence of the wild animals all around you.

'Could you have misheard?' asked Kiran.

Molly also told us that her gran says that when you are stuck in an old people's home gone at the knees and not even able to get out to the shops to choose your own knitting wool then you have plenty of time to Regret. And the things you regret most are the things you didn't do, not the things you did.

'I think that is very true and sad and pathetic,' said Molly.

'Your gran wasn't sad and pathetic last time we went round,' pointed out Kiran. 'She was watching Sky Sports and not regretting anything.'

'I was talking about *usually*,' said Molly patiently. 'That time wasn't usual. Nottingham Forest had just scored. She can't count on it happening very often.'

'She should support a better team,' said Kai. 'Then she could. What about Man U?'

'Yes, what about Man U?' agreed Kiran. 'It would be more sensible, you've got to admit.'

Molly clearly did not intend to be sidetracked because she agreed straight away that her grandmother should be ordered to desist from her lifetime's support of Nottingham Forest and turn instead to Manchester United, and then she went back to her original preoccupation of Only at Night.

With particular reference to the Zoo.

The Zoo and Molly's Impossible Plan and the Reason Why When Molly Said, 'Promise You Will Help, Please Promise You Will Help!' Kiran and I Should Not Have Said, 'Of Course We Will!', We Should Have Said, 'Help You With What?'

I have known since Monday what Molly was planning. Or dreaming. And I knew she was quite serious, because Molly is always quite serious, but I didn't really realize (I mean, *really* realize)

    she actually

    completely

totally

meant it.

'Yes well,' said Kiran crossly. 'You *should* have realized! Where else around here are there going to be any sort of magnificent even slightly wild animals around you at night?'

Last Sunday, while I was enjoying Snow White Christmas Pudding, guess what Molly was doing? Homework? No. Recorder practice? No. Laminating autographs? No.

Molly was on a reconnaissance trip to the Zoo.

'The arctic fox enclosure is completely deserted,' she said. 'They've been gone all year. Grass and bushes have grown up everywhere and their shed is empty. It will be the perfect place. Anyone could get over the wire, it is not even as high as me.'

'Is she saying what I think she's saying?' asked Kai in utter amazement.

'Yes,' said Kiran, and she described Molly's awful plan in all its ridiculous David-Attenborough-fuelled space-blanketed detail.

This was a great mistake. Kai's subsidiary interest in practical jokes suddenly became a major total enthusiasm and he said, 'Oh fantastic! Brilliant! The boys will help! I can't believe Molly thought of all that on her own!'

Molly blushed happily.

'I wish I could do it too,' said Kai. 'Only I am grounded from sleepovers and parties for the rest of the year because of that phone call I shouldn't have made on Mum's birthday.'

'That's an idea!' exclaimed Kiran. 'Let's get ourselves grounded right away, Rose!'

'Oh!' said Molly and got tears in her eyes and said that we had promised. And that this was the first not boring thing she had ever thought of and it was being ruined.

And yesterday I had agreed with everything she said and so now why was I changing my mind?

And perhaps we are scared of getting Mr Spencer in trouble and that's why we are being so horrible.

And other similar things.

With little sniffs in between.

'I don't remember agreeing to anything yesterday,' I said a bit crossly, because emotional blackmail does make you cross.

'You did!' said Kiran. 'And when I tried to warn you you took no notice and talked about your bedroom walls.'

'Well, anyway,' I continued. 'How could it ever really happen?'

'Mrs Shah said it was amazing what Class 6 could accomplish when they worked together as a team,' sniffed

Molly, and Kai said, 'Stop being rotten to Moll! I thought you were supposed to be her friends!'

Then the bell went because it was one o'clock (eight a.m. in New York), the end of lunch, and time for Mr Spencer to attempt to teach us Vectors.

Whatever they may be.

'Kai and Molly!' said Kiran as we walked home from school together after this unhappy experience. 'Do you think so? Or not?'

'Don't know.'

'One of my aunties met one of my uncles at junior school,' said Kiran.

'Then what?'

'Nothing for about a million years and then they got married.'

'Oh.'

'So that was good until she got run over. Then not so good. Although. . .'

'What?' I asked, because Kiran was suddenly speechless with giggles. 'What?'

'She still haunts him.'

We doubled up and staggered, leaned against walls and moaned at the pain in our ribs.

'I'm going to live in the Zoo-hoo-hoo,' sang Kiran madly. 'I've made up my mind. Suddenly. I've decided that I need locking up for my own safety. How many times can you spin round without falling over?'

'About one.'

'Would you mind very much coming back to the school gates and starting walking home all over again so that I can see if I can go the whole way spinning?' asked Kiran, spinning.

No, I wouldn't mind doing that.

'You'll have to steer me across the road because the lollipop lady will have gone.'

Of course.

'Then if you liked you could come to tea at my house. We've got our Christmas trees up.'

'Trees?'

'One in the garden,' said Kiran, revolving slowly past two shocked old ladies. 'One on the upstairs landing outside my bedroom and a Six-Foot Deluxe Fibre-Optic Norwegian Fir in the lounge.'

Kiran's family is all ready for Christmas. It could happen tomorrow and they would not be disturbed. Christmas cards are arranged in beautiful tidy fans on the walls of the hall and kitchen. The Christmas trees are wonderful. The one in the garden is covered in tiny lanterns, all colours of the rainbow. Upstairs the tree on the landing is decorated entirely with chocolate and red-and-white candy canes. In the lounge the Deluxe Fibre-Optic Norwegian Fir has piles of presents waiting beneath it already.

The whole house is incredibly tidy.

When I got home I arranged some of our Christmas cards in fans. It took a lot of Sellotape.

Later I took the housekeeping jar to bed with me and counted the contents to see if we could afford a Six-Foot Deluxe Fibre-Optic Norwegian Fir.

Probably not.

Thursday 14th December

Oh Bloody Bloody Hell!

I did not mean to fall asleep with the housekeeping jar but somehow I did. There happens to be a vast accumulation of pennies in it at the moment, and in the dark the lid unscrewed itself so that I woke in the very early morning to find I had been sleeping on a pile of coins.

'Like a dragon,' remarked Indigo, popping his head round the door for a moment. 'Can I have a bit of your hoard for the bus? You don't need to get up yet, Rose, it's still really early.'

'Good,' I said. I had a favour to ask Saffron and I wanted to catch her before she began her early morning acceleration of shower and hair and mirrors and bags and I-only-have-time-for-toast and lip-gloss and Rose-have-you-got-my-mobile, say-bye-to-Eve-for-me, I-don't-know-when-I'll-be-home-but-I-will-be-home . . .

. . . . *zoom*

. . . . . *out of the door.*

Sometimes Saffy moves so fast that it is weird that you don't see smoke.

My plan was to catch her before she got started.

'Gosh Rose, go *away*!' moaned Saffy when I began to gently joggle her awake (I notice that she sleeps with her back to the drum kit). 'It's still the middle of the night.'

'No it isn't,' I told her. 'Indigo's left already to do his papers and I can hear Mummy making coffee in the kitchen. Saffy, did you know it was twelve shopping days until Christmas last Saturday and now it's Thursday and we still haven't got a Christmas tree? Kiran has three, one outside and one upstairs and a Six-Foot Deluxe Fibre-Optic Norwegian Fir in the lounge.'

Saffron got under her pillow and said,

'Just buzz off, please, Rose?'

'So I thought,' I said, lifting the pillow slightly off her head so that she could hear, 'we could go shopping after school and get one too. I've got the housekeeping jar.'

'Rose,' said Saffron, 'I don't care if you've got the pin number of the Bank of England, no way is a six-foot deluxe fibre-optic Norwegian fir becoming part of my world.'

I thought she might say that.

'What about an ordinary Christmas tree then?' I asked.

'Since when do I have to organize the rotten Christmas tree?' complained Saffy.

Since Daddy went to London and Mummy got ill and Caddy went away to hunt for Michael and never came back. As Saffy knew perfectly well and I didn't have to explain.

Saffy is not daft.

A poignant silence is usually enough.

'Oh, all right,' she groaned with her eyes shut. 'I'll do it. But not today. I'm meeting Oscar straight after school today.'

'Tomorrow?'

'Tomorrow's impossible because it's Friday. Saturday.'

'Saturday?'

'Saturday afternoon (I'm going with Sarah to get her hair done in the morning). About two-ish.'

'I wish it could be sooner.'

'Saturday afternoon will be perfect,' said Saffron firmly. 'Then you can fling on the bling on Saturday night with Eve and Indy and that will be nice for you . . .'

'And you and Sarah?'

'Sorry. *Not* and me and Sarah.'

'But. . .'

'Rose, I *know* you would like the whole family decorating the tree together with deep snow on the ground outside and stars like white flowers blossoming in the Christmas sky and Tiny Tim's crutches propped up in the corner . . . Stop glaring! . . . And Little Donkey Little Donkey with its heavy load walking in the air with the Snowman and that boy in the grandad dressing gown . . . I'm going to make you smile, give in, stop fighting it! . . . And Santa hanging mistletoe over a blissful turkey that died ready-roasted of its own free will. . .'

I gave in and smiled.

'. . . but it just cannot happen. On Saturday Sarah and I are doing an all-night babysit for our Spanish teacher. We promised ages ago, and she doesn't charge for Extra Spanish and it's the only way we can say thank you. *Therefore* I have to tell you that on this particular tree-adorning issue poignant silences will have no effect *at all! GOOD GRIEF IS THAT THE TIME?*

It was the time.

And so poor Saffy leaped out of bed, tripped over my legs and fell hard on her face into a very sharp sticking out part of David's drum kit.

I heard her gasp.

Then she doubled up and sat down suddenly on her bed and I knew it was going to be awful.

'Oh bloody bloody hell,' she moaned (thus ending a

lifetime of never swearing). 'I daren't look. You'll have to. Put the light on, Rose.'

So I did, and after the dazzled pain of going from 0–100 watts had left my eyes, I looked.

There was a split like the slice of a very sharp knife above Saffy's right eye.

About as long as my little finger.

And so deep that you could see the layers of wrapping that made her face. Creamy skin and pinky purple flesh and then a smooth unnatural blueish white.

Is that the colour of Saffron's bones?

Yes.

At first Mummy thought the trouble was with me, because Saffron was perfectly quiet, bound with silence, and I was the one who was screaming. But then I pointed and Mummy saw.

There wasn't really much blood.

'Ice,' said Mummy, 'and then hospital. Casualty. Don't panic. Oh Saffy darling!'

'It's all my fault, it's all my fault, it's all my fault,' I whimpered (unhelpfully, but don't forget I had seen the extent of the damage and I was suffering from shock. Everyone knows that humans are rigid with bones but you do not expect to actually see them).

'Frozen peas,' said Mummy, not looking at all well. 'Or something. Hurry, Rose, while I help Saffy on with something warm. Bill come home.'

Daddy. He does not come home often, although far more since his girlfriend dumped him.

That was my fault too.

Our car doesn't always start first time, but this morning it did and as soon as we had scratched enough ice off the windows for Mummy to be able to see out we were off. And five minutes later we were stopped by a police car which overtook us from behind with all lights flashing and then ground to a halt in front.

Oh.

Two policemen got out, one old and hideous, one young and beautiful. Mummy buried her face in her hands because she has an irrational fear of law and order. I cannot think why. She never does any crimes.

However, despite her fear, Mummy is always very brave in a crisis. Her face was in her hands for only the smallest moment. Then she said, 'Look after Saffy, Rose,' and climbed out and started negotiations with Old and Hideous while Young and Beautiful rummaged around in the police car boot in an urgent kind of way, looking for something.

Handcuffs, I wondered. Ball and chain? Portable flat-pack prison?

Nearly.

Fancy breathalysing someone at 8.45 a.m. on a freezing cold Thursday morning.

'Why?' I demanded, climbing out and shouting so furiously that O and H actually answered me.

'Weaving about all over the road.'

No, she wasn't! I'm sure she wasn't. I was there and I'd have noticed.

'Not everyone realizes,' continued O and H, in a very loud voice that attracted the interest of several people passing by, 'that a heavy session the night before can—'

I am sorry that I tried to kick him.* It is not the way I've been brought up to behave, but poor Mummy. She has drunk nothing stronger than herbal tea for days. And Saffy was bleeding.

* NB if you are twelve and crying and try to kick a policeman you don't get arrested. You get glanced at.

'Bleeding?' asked Young and Beautiful, who had been hanging around looking very bored. 'Oh dear,' and he went round to our car and opened a door to peer in at Saffy. She was holding a bag of frozen baby Brussels sprouts and chestnuts to her forehead because I had not been able to find peas and she looked faint and furious and completely unencouraging.

'Very seasonal,' commented Y and B, grinning at the Brussels sprouts. 'And what have you been doing, then?'

'Leave her alone!' I shouted, crying and punching him (which I now also regret although I don't think he felt it). 'She walked into an upside-down drum kit and it cut her right down to the bone!'

'Move the veg!' commanded Y and B. 'Turn to the light! Oh yes. Oh very nasty. Oh dear.'

We drove to the hospital under police escort, with the police car in front flashing its lights like we were a big important emergency. I suppose I should have enjoyed it.

But I didn't.

Once in Casualty the police escort deserted us, although not before Y and B had given his phone number on a card to Saffy. 'You wouldn't believe the head injuries I've seen,' he remarked, breathing too much. 'Yours is nothing, darling.'

'That was the worst chat-up line I ever heard,' said Saffy, tossing away his card as soon as he had gone. Then she retired to be grumpy behind her Brussels sprouts while Mummy closed her eyes, leaned back in her red plastic chair and went into a trance. I went and fiddled with the horrible Accident and Emergency Christmas tree. It was such a long morning that I had time to rearrange all the decorations and make a fairy for the top out of two plastic cups and Mummy's lipstick.

Hours and hours later we climbed into the car to drive back home. Now instead of vegetables Saffy's head was covered in a big white dressing. Under the dressing were stitches, real ones, not the Sellotape ones they use for lesser injuries.

'Good as new!' announced the nurse who did the deed, but Saffy didn't look good as new. She looked awful. Her hair was streaked with dried blood and her front was splattered with Brussels sprout and chestnut juice that had somehow leaked from the bag as it thawed. I am often dirty and sometimes bandaged but I always look more or less the same. It is not like that for beautiful people. Things show up on them more, and injuries look much worse. They find this very hard to put up with and it makes them snarl at their relations.

Then when their relations are upset they're sorry.

But it doesn't last long.

Driving home with Saffy was like driving home with a repentant crocodile with short-term memory problems.

'Shut it, Rose!' she snapped, nearly every time I spoke, and then, 'Sorry, sorry, sorry!'

Home was so gloomy I went to school and nobody tried to stop me. I wished I hadn't when I got there. Lunch had just finished, everyone was wearing paper cracker hats and there was a smell of turkey and stuffing in the air as thick as fog.

'You missed Christmas dinner, Rose!' exclaimed Molly, rushing at me. 'Where have you been? Are you ill? Kiran saved you two crackers and Mr Spencer says we have tests in Science, Maths and Literacy this afternoon . . .'

Just when you think a day can't get any worse it does. There was a message for me on the answerphone when I got back.

'Hi there, Permanent Rose.'

Tom in New York, and I'd missed it. I felt like lying on the floor and howling. I *would* have done, I was just about to, when the telephone rang again.

'Tom?'

'Rose?' said Daddy.

'Oh bloody bloody hell!' I wailed.

'ROSE!' thundered Daddy.

*

'I hope you like defrosted pizza marinaded in melted ice cream,' said Indigo. 'The freezer door's been open all day.'

'Why sleep with a drum kit if you don't have to?' asked Sarah when she came round to survey the damage that evening. 'I have two beds in my room and pop stars all over the walls. Mum would love to have you, and Eve wouldn't mind you coming, would you, Eve?'

'I suppose not,' said Mummy, unhappily.

Saffy even took her angel. It has stood on her windowsill for so long the room looks empty without it.

'How can a room containing a full-size drum kit look empty?' said Saffron, when I said this.

I don't know, but it does.

'Is Saffy not needing her room just now then?' asked David, in a speculative kind of way.

'Hate the shed,' murmured Mummy, swallowing Paracetamol at the kitchen door.

WHAT?

'I hate

my shed

I said,'

said Mummy.

153

Friday 15th December

The Unlovable Mr Spencer followed by:
Medical News
Bad News
and
Totally Awful News.
I Will Start With the Unlovable Mr Spencer

This morning the UMS read out the results of the three tests he gave us yesterday. Here in Class 6, until Mr Spencer took control of our happiness, test results were read out in alphabetical order which meant I always came first.

Not any more. The UMS read them out in order of marks. I came last in all three.

'Obviously I anticipated a substantial drop in standard when I moved you away from Kiran,' he said. 'But I must admit I didn't expect such an abysmal plummet. What are we to do with you? Yes, Girl-at-the-Back?'

'It is not really fair,' said Molly (who had not yet noticed that things are *not* fair), 'because Rose had a very bad morning yesterday and she missed Christmas lunch except for her crackers and had to do the tests straight after and I think you ought to be . . . ought to be . . . ought to be . . .'

'Mmmm?' enquired Mr Spencer, licking his teeth.

'Nice,' said Molly.

'Nice?'

'And give her another chance!'

NO!

Across the room from me Kiran caught my eye. She knew what was coming, and so did I.

'What an excellent idea!' said Mr Spencer, smiling enormously into Molly's alarmed blue eyes.

I could see how sorry Molly was, but it took two break times, lunch and most of PE to work through those papers again.

'The man is a monster,' said Kiran, grabbing me after school. 'Come on, Rose, hurry! I bet you haven't packed anything yet!'

'Packed?'

'For Monday! The class trip! Our wild night out! And by the way, Molly and I have told our mothers we will be spending the night with you (which is perfectly true of course). And we thought you could tell yours you are spending it with us (which obviously you will be). Oh don't look so muddled, Rose! You can't have forgotten everything! Arctic foxes' cosy shed? Space blankets? David Attenborough? Wake up!'

'But what will happen on Monday night if our families ring each other up to check where we are?'

'Of course they won't,' said Kiran, cheerfully hurrying me through the puddles. 'Why should they? They're used to us having sleepovers. We've stopped at each other's loads of times before. Wear very warm clothes, Rose, and bring lots of food. And a torch. I'm going to the library tomorrow to see if they have any books about identifying animals by their roars . . .'

Kiran had gone mad and I told her so.

'You've forgotten what school trips are like!' I said. 'They take lists! Registers! It really can't work, Kiran. They'll take a register on the coach going, and another before they come home.'

'Kai's got that covered,' said Kiran smugly.

'And we won't just have Mr Spencer with us. There'll be another teacher as well. There's always two.'

'No problem. It's that tiny little student who doesn't know anyone's names.'

'The Zoo people,' I said desperately, 'will catch us in the morning! Then what?'

'Then we'll have done it so it won't matter a bit,' replied

Kiran, hopping cracks in the pavement. 'Come *on*, Rose!'

But I wouldn't come on. I stomped through the wet until we got to my house, and I didn't invite Kiran in. But as she walked away (backwards because she was going to see if she could make it home backwards) I thought of one more thing, and I called after her, 'You and Molly could do it by yourselves! I don't have to come. You don't need me!'

'We don't *need* you,' replied Kiran, laughing at my grumpy face. 'We *want* you! Dope!'

I have to admit, it is nice to be wanted.

Medical News

Mummy's illness has got new tablets and a name.

Bronchitis.

So now she will be better in nearly no time.

She says.

Bad News

David's drum kit is no longer in bloodstained pieces all over Saffy's bedroom. It's been reassembled the right way up.

There are some words, Indigo told me yesterday, that you can only say when you have very recently split your head open down to the bone on somebody else's drum kit. Otherwise don't even think about trying it, Rose.

So I will just have to call this:

Totally Awful News

My lovely misty pinewood full of Christmas trees, the nicest drawing I ever did.

Vandalized!!!!!!

Gluey glitter in the snow. Wrapping paper decorations on the branches. Hologram strings of tinsel loops. A smallish reindeer with a red plastic nose and unnaturally jointed legs and a large two-dimensional cotton-wool snowman grinning under my silvery moon.

Who has done this thing to me? Saffron and Sarah as a terrible joke? Mummy, in a spell of bronchitis-induced insanity? Indigo, in revenge for the time I bit him when I was two years old?

I don't think so.

David.

I was speechless with unhappiness.

Later, while Indigo was preparing/ruining supper for everyone (meatballs and tinned spaghetti served with extra spaghetti. V. nice if only Indigo leaves it as that and does not try to add rotten vitamins. And flavour. Which he is terribly prone to do) he tried to cheer me up by talking about Tom.

'Can't you really guess what he asked for for Christmas?'

'No.'

'He told me.'

'Yes, because he likes you better than me. Oh, Indigo! Don't put that stuff in!'

Too late. Indigo had added a whole handful of what looked like the contents of the vacuum cleaner bag. Disgusting Dried Mixed Mediterranean Herbs.

'Now it's going to taste weird,' I said crossly.

'Now it's going to taste nice,' said Indigo. 'Come on! Tom's Christmas present! Do you want me to give you a clue?'

No.

'You're in an awful mood.'

Yes I am.

'Don't forget you are going to have to say thank you to David!'

WHAT!

'Or else he'll be upset. It was very kind of him. And clever. I thought he'd just gone upstairs to fix his drum kit.'

His *bloodstained* drum kit! I wonder if he washed the blood off.

How callous if he did.

Or if he didn't.

I mentioned this.

159

'Go and check,' suggested Indigo, which I knew was just a plot to get me out of the kitchen. It wasn't going to work either. A whole tin of yucky sweetcorn has already been tipped into the meatball saucepan, as well as the Mediterranean vacuum cleanings. Indigo thought I hadn't noticed but I had and now I was On Guard.

'*I* thought David did well!' continued Indigo. 'He must have planned it really carefully to do it all so quickly . . .'

(He was trying to make David sound like some kind of Father Christmas but it wasn't working with me.)

'. . . It's not even as if he is any good at Art.'

Oh, tell me about it, Indigo! And what is that you are holding behind your back?

I don't believe it!

Sun-dried tomatoes!

I made a grab, but too late. Indigo held them above my head where I could not reach and poured them in from a height.

'Stop it!' I yelled. 'Why do you have to keep putting vegetables into everything?'

'Jamie Oliver,' said Indigo.

I shouted that I was totally fed up of Indigo's friends ruining everything. First my bedroom and now my supper.

'OK, we'll make a bargain,' said Indigo, when he had

stopped laughing. 'You be nice to David and I'll miss out the French beans . . .'

No. French beans (horrible poisonous things) don't frighten me. They're easy to pick out and leave on the side of your plate.

'. . . and the garlic purée and the freshly ground black pepper . . .'

Garlic purée!

He never would.

Black pepper.

He might.

'. . . and you can have grated cheese on top.'

Oh, all right.

I'll be nice to David.

But I won't say thank you.

And I may

Run away

To the Zoo.

Saturday 16th December

Reading and Love

'I've noticed David doesn't seem to be having a very good time at home lately,' remarked Indigo.

Indigo, I realized, knew nothing of the camp in the dead grandad's attic. All the same, he shook his head as he added, 'Poor old David.'

What about poor old me? I'm not having a very good time at home lately either. David is always at our house.

Drumming.

Drumming was the sound that woke me up this Saturday morning. Very quiet (but not quiet enough) drumming. It sounded very much like the drumming of someone who hopes you will get up and say to them, 'I loved my surprise, David. My decorated forest. You were so kind. It is so bright. Thank you.'

Hmmm.

However (good news) I am not in an awful mood anymore! I am in a very happy mood.

162

This is because it is Christmas Tree Day.

I don't really want a Six-Foot Deluxe Fibre-Optic Norwegian Fir. I would be just as happy with one of the chunky little real trees they sell on the Saturday market. They have roots on, and if you look after them carefully they will really grow. Sarah's family have one that they bring in every year. It has become so large that the only place it will fit is at the foot of the stairs in the hall. While it's there a sweet green smell fills the house.

Lovely.

I was all ready for our Christmas tree. I had emptied out a big tub that used to hold guinea-pig food to stand it in, and I had found a set of fairy lights and tested them and they still all worked. On my way home from school on Thursday I bought silver and gold angel hair. (Angel hair reminds me of Caddy.)

The boxes of decorations were waiting in the living room, together with a roll of red-and-gold striped paper for covering the guinea-pig tub. My only trouble was waiting until two o'clock in the afternoon, when Saffy and Sarah would be free. It was only just after nine and David was drumming in the next room. I was stuck in my bedroom and I had nothing to do.

If I owned a mobile phone I could have called Kiran

or Molly. They each have their own (lucky things). They don't have to borrow other people's and get moaned at for flattening the battery and changing the ringtones.

But I didn't have a phone and the nearest place one might be was the kitchen and I was not going to get up and hunt for it and risk being caught by David. Anyway, I guessed Kiran and Molly were busy. Kiran was probably at the library, looking for a book about identifying animals by the roars. And Molly had probably gone with her. Molly is a very library kind of person. She has had her own library card since she was three months old.

I wish Molly and Kiran had seen my forest bedroom before David ruined it. The lighter the morning grew, the more I could not help seeing the destruction of my lovely winter trees.

I thought this was supposed to be a good day. Quick, think of something to do!

What can you do when you are trapped in a room with unbearable walls?

No communication with the outside world.

Imprisoned (unless you can make up your mind to get up and Be Nice) by the Drummer in the Next Room.

Read a book.

I had a book. Following her huge success with *Where*

the Wild Things Are Sarah had become very excited and increased her efforts. Recently she had produced:

The Wind in the Willows.

'More wild things,' Sarah had said when she pulled it out of her bag. 'Mum thought you would love it. Lovely pictures. Look!'

I looked at a large rat in an old-fashioned suit.

Oh dear, rats. Dressed or caged, they're not for me.

'Oh well,' said Sarah, taking it back again. 'Never mind. Try this.'

Tales from Camelot.

'That's not actually a real book,' I explained to Sarah when I returned it a few days later. 'It is a copy of another, much better book, called *Le Morte D'Arthur,* written by a man called Thomas Malory more than five hundred years ago.'

'I didn't realize you were a scholar of Medieval Literature,' Sarah had said, laughing, and she had taken away the glossy new *Tales from Camelot* and given me instead a very tatty paperback called *The Once and Future King.*

'It is too thick and the print is too small,' I'd protested.

'Rubbish,' said Sarah. 'If you can read *Morte D'Arthur* for goodness' sake, you can read that. Stop moaning and get on with it.'

I can't read *Morte D'Arthur* and never could: the bits I knew about had been read to me by Indigo. Still, I had to do something to pass the long long stretch of morning before it was time to go Christmas tree shopping. So I picked up *The Once and Future King* and found the first page.

Kay was there, and Arthur and Sir Ector. They were talking and I could hear. It was like walking into a strange room and finding it unexpectedly full of friends.

It was hours later when I put that book down again. The drumming had stopped and the telephone was ringing and my brain had the sort of dazed feeling you get when you wake from a very vivid dream.

So *that's* what they were talking about, Saffy and Sarah, and Kiran and Molly and Miss Farley and Daddy and Indigo and Sarah's parents and even the Unlovable Mr Spencer.

Reading!

Down in the kitchen the telephone was still ringing and when I picked it up I found that it was David's mother, and she was in her usual very grumpy mood. It had been summer in the ancient greenwood of *The Once and Future King*, but it was definitely winter here.

'Where's David?' she demanded, with no preliminary hellos or how are yous, or anything like that. 'What's he been doing?'

'Earlier he was drumming,' I said, 'but now I think he's Out. Would you like me to give him a message?'

'Message indeed!' said David's mother, and then there was a bit of silence and then she said,

'I suppose he thinks he's clever!'

(Whatever mad delusions David has I am pretty sure they don't include thinking he is clever, but I didn't argue.)

'I suppose he thinks I don't know he's hiding over there!'

(Good grief! Can she know about the attic camp at dead Grandad's?)

'Skulking round at yours . . .'

(No. She doesn't know. Phew!)

'Yes, you can give him a message, if you please. You can tell him we want that key back. His grandad's key. He knows the one. We've not forgot he's got it. There's new people coming in.'

Oh dear. That's terrible. Poor old David.

'And while you're passing on messages you may as well tell him that we've booked Spain for Christmas . . .'

Spain! *Spain for Christmas!* Oh, lucky, lucky David! Why did I ever waste a second being sorry for him?

'Oh, it will be lovely!' I exclaimed. 'Oh, I wish it was me! Will there be sea? Will it be sunny?'

'That's what we're paying for,' she agreed, slightly less grumpily.

'David will absolutely love it!'

Whether David would love it or not, said David's mother, is neither Here Nor There, it's no affair of his, he's made his bed and must lie on it and anyway money doesn't grow on trees.

In other words, he's not invited.

'I have heard of people like you on the News!' I shout at David's mother.

Which doesn't help.

David's mother doesn't love him. Or if she does, it is in a very strange way, more strange than any way I have ever known myself. Not that mothers don't love their children in some pretty weird ways, I've noticed. For instance, Kai's mother. She loves him by making him make public apologies to the emergency services. And Molly's is even weirder. Molly's mother loves her by education: school lessons, swimming lessons, ballet lessons, music lessons, computer club, gym club, library club and (most important, see **Monday 18th December**) Brownies. (Molly's mother is an actual Brownie leader which is called a Brown Owl – nothing to do with Harry Potter.) Molly has files of certificates to prove that she can do things like turn one-handed cartwheels, remember arpeggios up to Grade 3, write 500 words on My Favourite Book and pick up a rubber brick from the bottom of the swimming pool in a depth of more than 1.5 metres.

And yet poor Molly thinks she is boring. Which isn't fair. I cannot do any of those things (I can do a cartwheel but not one-handed) and yet I don't think I'm boring.

I said this once to Molly, and I told her that whenever she felt particularly boring she should go and read her certificates.

'But don't you think,' asked Molly anxiously, 'that would be quite a boring thing to do, Rose?'

Kiran doesn't have certificates because her mother loves her by cleanness. Kiran is fantastically clean. She has a bath and hair wash every night, and a shower every morning and three sets of clean clothes a day: school clothes, playing clothes and pyjamas. It gives her a look of sparkling purity. But anyone who spends more than half an hour with Kiran finds out that although she may give the appearance of radiating white light, in reality she should be covered in warning signs.

My mother loves us by living in the shed to save us from

germs and by staying friends with Daddy.

Sarah's mother loves Sarah by keeping the freezer full of food for her friends and having tantrums about her piercings (ears, nose and – wicked, wicked Sarah – tummy button).

But I don't think that David's mother loves him in any way at all and I told Mummy this when we had Saturday breakfast-lunch together (Sugar Puffs and pizza for me, orange juice and antibiotics for Mummy).

'Poor woman,' said Mummy, not seeming at all jealous of even Christmas in Spain (even though she herself, between illness and work, will probably be spending Christmas in the shed). 'Poor thing. I can't imagine how she must feel.'

'What about poor David?' I asked indignantly.

'It is terrifically hard work being a mother,' said Mummy.

Oh really! I have vacuumed twice this week, and I unpacked all that shopping! And Saffy and Indigo have done nearly all the cooking lately.

Huh.

'What are you doing this afternoon, Rose?' asked Mummy, dragging herself up to go back to her cosy shed.

'Shopping for Christmas trees with Saffy.'

'Trees?' asked Mummy. 'I think one will be enough. Do try not to pick a too big one, won't you, darling?'

'What's too big?'

'Suppose we say, no taller than you?'

No taller than me! What kind of a Christmas tree is no taller than me?

'They so often seem OK outside and then look enormous when you get them indoors,' explained Mummy.

Since when was I enormous? And what if all the trees for sale turn out to be taller than me?

'Oh,' said Mummy. 'It wouldn't matter too much. I'm sure there is a very nice little white tinsel one up in the attic somewhere.'

I know she's ill, but this is not the reply a perfect mother should make. A perfect mother should say, 'Then buy an enormous one, and we will move out a chair or two to make room.'

'Small is beautiful,' said Mummy, unperfectly. 'Anything very big would be as bad as another drum kit.'

'It has to be big enough to get the presents underneath,' I said crossly.

'Well, darling . . .' said Mummy vaguely, 'that needn't be huge, need it? I wouldn't have supposed . . .'

And I bought her that lovely mug! Saying WORLD'S BEST EVER MOTHER.

I feel like changing it.

Sunday 17th December

I am ENEMIES With ALL My Family
and also
The Ridiculous Events of Late Last Night

I am ENEMIES With ALL My Family

The first thing that anyone coming into our house would notice is that there is

NO CHRISTMAS TREE.

This morning (Sunday) Caddy telephoned. She said, 'What is absolutely your most favourite name in the world?'

'*It is all very well for you!*' I yelled at her and banged down the phone.

Ever since I can remember Caddy has been asking that question. Parades of hamsters and guinea-pigs have passed through this house, all of them honoured with Absolutely Most Favourite Names in the World chosen at solemn meetings at the kitchen table, the Nameless One on a newspaper in the middle, awaiting the verdict.

Joseph, Blossom, Balthazar, Merry, Pippin and Frodo. Tiffany, Cocoa, Fudge and Smudge. Darcey Bussell the guinea pig who spun in circles (it was something wrong with her brain), Sebastian, Clover and Madeline.

'Gosh, Rose!' said Caddy, ringing back. 'I only asked—'

'S'not like you ever took any notice of anything I want, anyway!' I shouted. 'Same as the rest of my useless horrible family. All you care about is beastly horrible rodents! So. Goodbye.'

Bang again.

The last hamster had been nearly bright yellow, but would she call it Buttercup?

No.

She said Buttercup was a cow's name.

I might as well just not exist around here.

'Darling, darling, Rose!' said Caddy (calling again). 'Of course I take notice of what you say—'

'Buttercup,' I growled, 'and don't say it's a cow's name because so was Clover and you didn't mind that. Buttercup. Buttercup. Buttercup.'

You can whack a telephone down quite hard without smashing it.

'Rose, darling, darling Rose, just listen. I can't—'

'Buttercup, Buttercup, Buttercup, Buttercup, Buttercup, Buttercup, Buttercup,' I said angrily, crying all over the phone.

'But Rose—'

'Buttercup,' I shouted, and did another bang with the receiver.

Actually, I can see a crack.

I waited and waited and waited for Saffron yesterday.

And waited.

And waited.

And waited.

Until it became the longest wait of my life.

And now I am utterly finished with Saffron for ever and ever.

And that is that.

Last night Indigo barged into my room and told me that I was being unreasonable.

And he said if I wanted a Christmas tree NOW I could have the tinsel one out of the attic. OR I could wait a bit longer and he would take me out to get a real one ASAP. He said this quite pleasantly, but I was not pleasant back.

So then Indigo got a bit ratty and looked around my bedroom walls and said, 'I hope you said something nice to David about all this.'

'Well I didn't.'

174

'Rosy Pose,' said Indigo in such a quiet way that I felt even worse than ever.

'I haven't seen David today, anyway,' I said crossly.

'He came round to do some drumming.'

'Yes, well, he went away again, before I was properly up. He doesn't *live* here, even though he pretends to his rotten mother that he does.'

'Of course he doesn't,' said Indigo. 'Well, maybe he did that one night he stopped here but he's back home again now.'

'He's not! And his mother wants his dead grandad's key back and she's going to Spain without him.'

'How do you know all that?' demanded Indigo.

'She telephoned.'

'And she thinks he's staying here?' asked Indigo, and then he said, 'Where *is* he then?' and hurried downstairs without waiting for an answer and started looking up the numbers of Patrick and Marcus and Josh, the people he knew David had stayed with before.

So I went down too, and I said, 'He's at his grandad's.'

'What?' said Indigo, and Mummy, who was in the room too, said, 'Rose?'

'He's at his dead grandad's, living in the attic.'

'Say that again!'

'David is at his dead grandad's house,' I repeated, speaking as though they were being very stupid. 'He is living in the attic and he has been there for days. He has a sleeping bag and a camping stove and candles. He cooks soup and plays the drums on empty boxes. He is perfectly all right.'

'*Perfectly all right?*' repeated Indigo, staring at me.

'How long have you known that, Rosy Pose?' asked Mummy, in a very shocked voice.

'Ages and ages,' I said.

The Ridiculous Events of Late Last Night

So then, even though it was nearly the middle of the night, and sleet was falling and Mummy's chest was hurting and everyone was exhausted and David would have been perfectly OK where he was for a bit longer, we had to get into the freezing cold car and drive to his dead grandad's house.

'That poor boy,' said Mummy, tears and other stuff streaming down her face. 'We do not know how fortunate we are. And to think we worried about a Christmas tree, Rose!'

We worried! What a cheek! Nobody worried except me.

*

Afterwards Mummy said that David's attic was the most desperate place she'd ever seen. I don't know why she thought that. It looked perfectly all right to me. Very tidy. Cooking things and a loaf and some tins lined up on one side. A towel and socks and stuff hanging from a line strung between two roof joists. His sleeping bag and his drum boxes and a little pile of Christmas presents that he scuffled hastily out of sight. Candles. A bucket of water in case of fire.

Everything you could possibly need.

Although I must say it was not as cosy as it sounded when he described it to me.

Well, it was not cosy at all.

It was extremely cold.

'It is freezing,' wheezed Mummy, having clambered up the attic trapdoor stairs. 'I think it is even colder than outside. Come on, Rose! You and I will wait in the car while the boys collect the bits and pieces and lock up. Try to be quick, both of you!'

Both of you! Didn't we just come to check that he was OK? Mummy made it sound like we were taking him home.

'Of course we are taking him home,' said Mummy,

turning the car heating up full and huffing on her fingers.

WHY? WHY? WHY? WHY? WHY?

Then, while we waited for Indigo and David, Mummy and I had a great big argument about whether it would be unforgivable not to take David home. It made Mummy cough a lot so I gave in.

'He can have Saffron's room while she is at Sarah's,' said Mummy. 'It will only be for a little while.'

But she didn't mean that. I know, because one minute later when David was in the car saying, 'I shouldn't come. I'm doing fine. I'll be all right. You don't want me,' etc etc she said, '*Of course* you should come. We want you very much. You are very very welcome to stay with us *for as long as you like!*'

'Isn't he, Rose?' she added.

'Oh yes,' I said.

After Indigo had poked me twice.

So now we have swopped Saffy for David, and I don't see how we will ever manage to get them swopped back, and that seems all wrong to me because (although I have finished with Saffron for good) after all, she is the one who lives here.

And so she should be here.

And David doesn't live here.

And so he shouldn't.

And now it is Sunday afternoon.

Daddy is in London, which has lost all its magic and where he personally is Burned Out.

Caddy is miles away, choosing names for guinea-pigs.

Michael is dodging us.

Mummy is resting on her bed, and do you know what she said before she went up? She said, 'I'm sorry you've quarrelled with Darling Saffy, Rose.'

Darling Saffy!

Indigo and David are cooking in the kitchen.

Darling Saffy is at Sarah's house. Good riddance too. I am never going to speak to her again and I will not listen to anything she says.

She lost her bag when she was in town yesterday morning.

Can't say I'm interested.

She panicked. And went back to everywhere she had been. In a flap.

Who cares?

And she didn't notice the time going by until LONG after two o'clock.

I did.

And then it was much too late.

Dear, dear.

Because it was babysitting time.

Huh.

She *did* try to explain, when she telephoned, but I wouldn't listen.

OH WELL HOW SURPRISING IS THAT?

I never have liked Sunday afternoons. There is something about them. They are colder and emptier than other times, and even if you are doing something nice you can't help knowing that it will soon all end and the next thing is Monday morning. But this particular Sunday afternoon was the worst I had ever had. I was very unhappy. What I felt like doing was yelling very nastily and crossly at someone, and when Daddy telephoned I had the chance to do this, and I made the most of it.

I shouted about Christmas trees and drum kits and bronchitis and Scrubbable Magnolia, and Sarah's big posh house and kind funny father who's always there, and horrible Mr Spencer, and attics and sheds and hamsters and long-life muffins.

I could have gone on for hours, and I would have done

except the handset of the telephone suddenly fell in half and I was afraid of getting an electric shock from the wires. But even the amount of shouting I had managed to complete did me good. I felt very brave after it all and I remembered that even if my family were useless I still had my lovely friends, Molly and Kiran.

I thought of Molly sticking up for me to horrible Mr Spencer, and Kiran walking backwards in the rain, and laughing and saying, 'We *want* you! Dope!'

'You've cheered up!' said Indigo, some time after supper (curried meatballs with apples in the curry sauce. Surprisingly edible, invented by David who was now – having begged for the privilege – washing up in the kitchen). 'Whatever are you stuffing into that bag? Have you seen my mobile and was it you who broke the receiver on the telephone? Where are you taking that torch? It's the only one that works!'

I didn't have to reply to any of these questions. Indigo was messing about with his guitar and concentrating on it much more than on me. Anyway, I knew he didn't really want any answers. It was just what Kiran calls Routine Interrogation of the Youngest Person Present and happens in all families. So I carried on with my packing until Mummy drifted in and started an antibiotic hunt.

(Owing to the David crisis she has forgotten to take her last three doses.)

(So we'll all know whose fault it is if she drops down dead.)

(Although they will probably find a way of blaming me.)

I was remarking about this very quietly to myself when Indigo woke up to the world.

'What are you muttering about, Rose?' he asked. 'I don't suppose you've said thank you to poor old David yet? And anyway, shouldn't you be in bed?'

Charming.

Not that I care. What a rubbish family. Thank goodness for my friends.

However, bed is a wonderful idea. I should be making the most of it, while I have a chance. Me and *The Once and Future King*, *The Hobbit* and *The Blue Fairy Book*. I have been going through the bookcase in Saffy's room. The top shelves are full of intellectual and gloomy paperbacks belonging to Saffron, but the bottom shelves are stuffed with books that used to belong to Caddy. I have started several of them already. I have learned to read, but nobody has noticed.

Monday 18th December

I Never Knew a Day Could Be So Long

Just before I slammed out of the house this morning I yelled to David (who was making tea for Mummy and clearing up the toast crumbs from Indigo's early breakfast and generally acting like he'd lived with us for ever), 'By the way you'd better tell my rotten family I won't be here tonight.'

'Where will you be then, Rose?' asked David.

'With Kiran.'

'Kiran?' repeated David (now tenderly bandaging the telephone with insulating tape).

'She's a girl in my class. Molly will be there too, she's another girl in my class.'

'So you're stopping the night at a girl called Kiran's house and so is another girl called Molly and I'm to tell your mum?' said David. 'I think *you* should.'

Then he went very bright red and said, 'I know what you're thinking.'

What?

'That I'm a good one to talk.'

No, actually I wasn't (although it's true).

'That's a very big bag you are taking to school today,' continued David (after an embarrassed pause). 'I s'pose it's your night things. I did think when you brought it down that it must be for something special.'

I really do think David would have been quite all right if we had left him in that attic. He has a suspicious mind! I've noticed it before. It is the result of his guilty past – he has done it all himself and so he recognizes the clues.

So although I was still not really speaking to him (and certainly not ready to thank him for the hideous destruction of my bedroom) I tried to encourage him not to suspect anything more by saying very calmly and slowly, 'Oh, I suppose it is a bit special, because as well as staying with Kiran and Molly, today is our class trip to the Zoo.'

Then I went quickly out of the door and along the street and I didn't look back and didn't look back and didn't look back until almost the last moment.

And then I did and David was waving.

Poor old David.

It might be the last time I see him.

If a lion escapes and eats me, for instance.

It is very hard to be nasty all the time, non-stop without

a tiny little break. I don't know how Mr Spencer keeps it up.

So I turned round and ran back to the house, with my bag bumping like agony on my back, bump, bump, bump, opened the back door and yelled into the kitchen.

'Thank you, David, for decorating my bedroom!'

And ran away again.

And didn't look back and didn't look back and didn't look back.

Until almost the last moment.

And there was David, smiling.

In the school entrance hall Mr Spencer was being effortlessly nasty to a group of six-year-olds who looked too happy. I slipped past him and into our classroom.

'You're here, you're here, you're here!' exclaimed Molly jumping round me and hugging me. 'Look, Kiran, she's come!'

Kiran slightly raised one eyebrow to show how pleased she was. She could not do more than this because movement wastes oxygen and she was passing the time until the coaches arrived by seeing how long she could go without breathing.

'One minute twenty-three,' she said, giving Molly and me a wrist each so that we could take her pulse. 'It is all a matter of concentration. Have I managed to slow my heart rate yet? They do it all the time in Tibet.'

'You're dead,' I told her. 'No pulse at all on my side. What about you, Mollipop?'

Molly the Brownie was silently moving her lips as she counted, her eyes on the clock.

'Seventy-two,' she announced.

'Maybe she's only half dead,' suggested Kai, who had been watching Molly very admiringly. 'Alive on Molly's side, but dead on Rose's. Come on, Rose, now you're here you can guard the door! I've got to talk to everyone about Strategy and Tactics.'

Kai's lifelong membership of Gold Team (now renamed, see **Wednesday 29th November**) and his inability to tell left from right (hence peripatetic nature of shoes) might lead you to think he was daft. Not so. Kai stood on Mr Spencer's desk and addressed Class 6 like a master criminal ordering his gang.

'You All Know Why I'm Here,' he began (and for one moment it sounded like a repeat of his Assembly speech on Why Not to Ring the Emergency Services on Your Mother's 40th Birthday). 'It is because of a very special plan inspired by the famous naturalist and broadcaster Mr David Attenborough . . .' (Molly clapped) '. . . and the famous school secretary Mrs Shah and also Molly who will be famous some day I am sure and her friends Kiran and Rose who I don't know about. Maybe, maybe not.' (Pause, during which everyone looked at Kiran and me and shook their heads.) 'For this plan to work,' continued Kai, 'it's really important that we should prevent Mr Spencer ever being able to get us properly counted. That's the key to our success. So, right from the beginning of the day he should be made to realize that it's impossible. The sooner he gives up trying the better and I think he will give up pretty quick because let's face it, he's not that bothered. This is how we're going to do it: keeping swopping jackets and hats . . .' (Kai flourished his hat so beautifully Molly sighed) '. . . and weave! Everyone has got to weave . . .' (Kai wove a bit on the table) '. . . Dodge about and never stand still. Move between groups all the time. If you find you are being stared at . . .' (Pause for ferocious staring) '. . . pick your nose. It makes them glance away. The student teacher who is coming with us is really small so tallest people squash up around her whenever possible. Also, *never* answer any question in your natural voice, *don't* call anyone you're talking to by name and in moments of crisis *Go For the Ball!*'

Kai whisked from a bag a bright orange basketball and held it triumphantly high. We all cheered like mad, Kai leaped down from the table, I forgot I was on guard, and then suddenly the ball went flying and there was a new voice in the room.

'WHO threw that ball?' roared Mr Spencer. They were his last indignant words before he (and the student teacher who had followed him) were submerged in a scrum of weaving criminals, all swopping hats, picking their noses and calling in strange high voices. By the time they reappeared the ball was gone, the student teacher was flattened against the whiteboard and Kai was leading the race for the coaches and the car park.

'He's a genius,' said Kiran to Molly as we squashed on to the coach, and Molly went pink.

It was one of those days that pass like a dream. Here are the things I remember most:

1. The murmur of gratitude that went all around the bus when Mr Spencer handed the register to the student teacher who passed it to Molly who gave it to Kai.

2. The chimpanzees *dressed*, watching telly and eating nuts on a red plastic sofa.

3. The enormous number of enclosures that appeared to be empty but, after prolonged and chilly scrutiny, turned out to be anything but.

4. How Mr Spencer and the student teacher gave up all pretence of supervision, slunk into the Smoking Permitted section of the Zoo Restaurant and stayed there all day drinking scummy cappuccinos. We took it in turns to monitor them. The restaurant was decorated to look like a jungle, and Mr Spencer (who had shamed us all by turning up in an army surplus camouflage jacket) blended into the plastic foliage very well indeed.

But the thing I remember most was the quietness.

All that day we in Class 6 had the Zoo more or less to ourselves. It's a big place, and we split up into little groups, and sometimes it was so quiet that you could imagine your little group was the only one there.

And then you would go round a corner and find that it wasn't, and that was a nice friendly feeling.

Molly and Kiran and I were a group, of course, and Kai was with some boys in another, but we met up quite often, and when the afternoon was nearly over and a misty purple greyness was making it harder and harder to see, Kai said to Molly, 'I'm on to it, Moll!' and the next time we went round a corner and felt like we were the only people in the whole place it was true and we were.

And they had really and truly gone without us.

So.

*

I admit I was a big coward when it came to climbing into the arctic foxes' enclosure. I let Kiran and Molly go first. I was afraid that, in spite of the tangled dead grasses and the overgrown bushes and the general look of uninhabitedness, it would turn out, like so many of the other enclosures, to be Anything But.

But it was OK.

Arctic foxes live on the arctic tundra in the wild, but in this country they live in large wooden sheds with bark floors. The sheds have doors with locks on but when the foxes are going to be away for a long time the zoo people don't bother to lock the doors.

So that was OK too.

And there we were, inside the arctic foxes' shed.

Anybody who wants to camp in an arctic foxes' shed on a cold December night should take with them, as their most important bit of equipment, an uncomplaining and fully loaded Brownie.

Molly unpacked:

One plastic ground sheet

One tartan picnic rug

Three space blankets

Three blow-up pillows

One first aid kit

One halogen torch (with lifetime guarantee)

Planet Earth: The Book of the Series (by Guess Who)

Digestive biscuits, cheese pre-cut into wedges, cereal bars, ham slices, two cucumbers, snap cards, three sealed magic beakers that would turn into hot chocolate when shaken and a Hallowe'en Mask of a rubbery skull face with red eye sockets given to her at the last moment by Kai. To be used should things get boring to liven up Kiran and me.

Kiran (who is not a Brownie but a part-time vegetarian) unpacked:

One fleecy blanket

One box of French Fondant Fancies

One six-pack of Coca-Cola

Twelve peppermint candy canes

Six Luxury Iced Mince Pies

One chocolate orange

One tub of Pringles

(Life is difficult, says Kiran, for vegetarians who are not keen on vegetables. Particularly if they don't much like nuts or cheese. In fact it is one long sugar rush. That is why she breaks down now and then and eats bacon sandwiches and chicken curry and sausages and steak.)

Kiran also brought three books:

The first was all about Man-Eating Tigers.

The second was a book of True Ghost Stories.

The third was an account of a plane crash in South America where half the passengers died and the other half (oh dear oh dear the poor vegetarians who survived but there was no other food so what could they do?).

Ate them.

Kiran chose these books because she had not been able to find anything in the library about identifying animals by their roars.

Pity.

I unpacked:

    Mummy's torch

    Indigo's mobile

    My dressing gown

    My pyjamas

    My slippers

    My spongebag

    Saffy's Mango and Orange Blossom shower gel

    The Blue Fairy Book and my Christmas card from Michael

I may become a Brownie.

Molly and Kiran laughed until they were nearly sick when they saw my packing. Kiran said I should go and hang my spongebag in the bathroom and when I got up to do this they absolutely howled.

(Later on Kiran did not think it half so funny that the arctic foxes hadn't got a bathroom.)

After we had unpacked we had a huge feast by torchlight. We had to do this because the food was taking up so much space on the ground sheet that we had hardly anywhere to sit. Anyway, we were very hungry, having only had Zoo Restaurant Jungle Fun Lunchboxes for lunch. So we ate as much as possible of everything, including both the cucumbers so that we did not get scurvy or any of the things Indigo's friend Jamie Oliver says non-vegetable eaters get wrong with them. Also we had a Coke each, except for Kiran, who had two.

It was very strange, but while we were eating I think we almost forgot where we were. And afterwards, while we were blowing up our pillows and arranging our bed (with the ground sheet and picnic rug underneath and a space blanket each and the fleecy blanket on top) we hardly remembered either. It was only when we lay down with our books and torches that we properly realized.

'It must be nearly midnight,' whispered Molly. 'Midnight at the Zoo!'

Then she looked at her watch and it was a quarter to six.

Life is very complicated in an arctic foxes' shed. There are some details I would rather not remember. They took ages and absorbed all our thoughts. Molly managed the best. But she only drank half her Coke.

Do you think it is quiet in a zoo at night when the visitors go home, and the Gift Shop and Restaurant people switch off the lights and lock the doors, and the last cars creak across the gravel out of the car park?

No.

Zoo animals behave very badly after dark. Especially monkeys. I don't know how they manage to get up in the morning. There was a monkey house right across the path from us, and we could hear them plain as plain, pushing each other about and banging on the windows. And something that sounded like a yak was kicking something that sounded like a drum. And sudden wild squawks came every few minutes, never from the same direction. And someone very large and close had a cough.

Not to mention the footsteps.

The footsteps might be nightwatchmen moving between their little hut places.

Or they might be Mr Spencer, come furiously back to look for us.

Or they might be something from one of the cages, got out. Caddy was always telling us admiring stories of animals who got out. Monkeys opening locks with sticks. Mountain lions who could leap higher than their fences, but kept their talents secret until after nightfall. Elephants' footprints found on the wrong side of the dry moat in the morning.

There was that coughing again.

Molly glanced up from one of Kiran's books and murmured, 'It's a tiger.'

'WHAT!'

'Tigers cough. It says so here.'

I jumped up and began barricading the door with our backpacks. Kiran said, 'There aren't any tigers at this zoo.'

'There's one,' said Molly. 'Coughing.'

'Well, I didn't see any tigers today,' said Kiran. 'Rose, did you see any tigers today?'

I shook my head.

'See!' said Kiran. 'No tigers. Good.'

'I didn't know you didn't like tigers,' said Molly in a rather hurt voice.

'I didn't *say* I didn't like tigers,' said Kiran, looking uneasily at my barricade. 'I just said there weren't any or we'd have seen them. Wouldn't we, Rose?'

Probably. Although I'm not sure, because actually, I saw hardly any of any kind of animal today. They were all hiding in the bushes, or on sofas watching telly. I even missed the elephants, and I know for a fact that there is a whole herd. So I carried on arranging my barricade, and as an extra precaution I tucked David Attenborough under my arm. I thought David Attenborough would be a good person to have on your side if there were loose tigers around.

Especially as Molly had the hardback edition.

I wished I knew where a tiger's weak point was.

I asked Molly, as casually as I could, because I didn't want to frighten her, if she happened to have any idea.

Molly said she thought she had read somewhere that they have very sensitive digestions.

Oh.

This means that if there is a tiger on the loose I am going to have to make him

Eat

David Attenborough.

Well,

If you ask me,

It's about time someone did.

It was now about half past seven, and very cold. To take our minds off Man-Eating Tigers, Kiran read us bits from her plane crash book.

Then I read them bits from *The Blue Fairy Book*.

And then we played Snap very quietly in the dark which was useless, especially as we were listening all the time for tigers.

'There are

NO tigers

Here!' growled Kiran.

'There may be only one,' said Molly fairly, and I said one was enough.

'Especially if it is on the loose,' I said.

'Of course it is not on the loose!' replied Molly a little impatiently. 'There is all sorts of special security in zoos.

Things can't just wander in and out of the cages and not get noticed.'

Well!

We did!

'When we go out for our midnight explore,' said Molly, 'we'll track which direction the coughs are coming from and see whether it really is a tiger.'

WHAT IS ALL THIS ABOUT GOING OUT FOR A MIDNIGHT EXPLORE?

Molly and Kiran said, 'Of course we are going out, that is the *whole idea*!'

'But let's not wait till midnight,' said Kiran. 'Let's go right now!'

I don't know if I fancy that.

Tiger hunting in the dark.

Now.

Somebody ought to stay and guard the shed.

So that is how I ended up with the best torch and all the blankets and *The Blue Fairy Book* and two Cokes in case I got thirsty (no thank you I am not drinking again until I am out of this) all by myself in an arctic foxes' shed just before Christmas at night in a zoo.

I could hear gnawing.

And I could hear monkeys.

Cars.

Faraway voices.

Wind in the bushes.

A howl, lots of howls, just like wolves.

Probably wolves.

And I thought, Oh what a long time I have been here! Surely Kiran and Molly will be back soon. What is there to see in a zoo in the dark?

That tiger has a terrible cough.

I think I can hear an aeroplane.

I'm sure I can hear a duck.

And I can definitely hear

Quite close

And getting closer

Footsteps.

Kiran and Molly's footsteps?

No.

Our plan to spend the night at the Zoo was doomed. It was doomed for two reasons:

1. We underestimated the inquisitiveness of our parents.
2. We forgot David.

*

It began to go wrong when Molly's mother telephoned our house to check that Molly had arrived safely and had everything she needed for the night. And although Indigo was out and Mummy was safely not answering in her shed, David was home.

David explained that not only was Molly not at our house, but also I (Rose) was spending the night at someone called Kiran's house, and he was sure I had told him that Molly would be there too.

So of course Molly's mother said she would ring Kiran's family at once, and she did and very soon she rang back to say nobody was there, but not to panic, because it was school trip day and we could very well be stuck in traffic on our way home. And she would just call school to find out.

As soon as she put the phone down David rushed out to the shed. He didn't waste any time trying to find a gentle way of breaking his news.

'Rose is missing!' he puffed. 'God it sounds terrible she never got back from her school trip and neither did two other little girls!'

And then, Mummy told us, the room – I mean shed – went all swimmy as if it was dissolving and she probably would have passed out completely if she hadn't heard

200

David's voice, saying, 'Mind, they might just be stuck in traffic, that's what one of the mothers said.'

At which timely remark Mummy recovered enough to do what she always does in a crisis, which is ring Daddy.

And Daddy, for whom London has lost all its magic, who had been worrying about us ever since my cross shouting phone call, who was Personally Burned Out and longing to come home, turned wonderful.

Daddy does this now and then. Saffy says that it's his ability to turn irresistibly wonderful that has allowed him to get away with so much.

'I'm on my way!' said Daddy, and it was true, they could hear him rushing round putting things into his pockets. 'I'm dropping everything, sweetheart . . .' *(Sweetheart!)* '. . . Call the police! Call school! Call the coach company! Call someone to come and be with you! I hate to think of you all alone!'

('I could make a cynical remark,' said Saffy, on hearing the account of all this, 'but I won't.')

'I've got David,' said Mummy (in response to my father's last, uncharacteristic announcement). 'So I'm not alone. He is being an Absolute Darling.' (David, when he reported this conversation to me, repeated the last bit about him being an absolute darling at least a hundred times.

Well.

Twice, anyway.)

'Call me the moment you hear anything,' continued Daddy. 'Call me anyway, Eve sweet!'

But Mum didn't call anyone. She had scarcely time to recover from all this irresistible wonderfulness (not to mention the shock of losing a daughter and gaining a husband) before Kiran's father telephoned.

'Stop panicking,' he said. 'Or anyway, stop panicking quite as much. I knew our Kiran was up to something. And Molly's mum checked around and found David Attenborough and two large cucumbers were missing and a note from Molly in the fridge. Which she popped round with and I'll read to you now. It says, "If you have noticed about the cucumbers you will have noticed about me too and I am quite all right doing something I have always wanted to do and we will not do anything to upset the animals and we have taken things to eat and things to keep warm from the Brownie Camp Cupboard and I will clean my teeth properly in the morning. Love Molly."'

So then, as Indigo later remarked, the game was up.

Kiran's father set off for the Zoo.

Daddy was called and told to drive much less fast

and get here safely (darling).

The Zoo were informed that three very young girls were thought to be loose in their grounds.

And people were sent to look for us at once.

One of them came my way.

That was the footsteps.

They had a torch and they called 'Hello! Hello! Don't be frightened!'

In a very familiar voice.

Thus (Oh, excellent word) Caddy and I met by torchlight in the brambly dark outside the arctic foxes' shed.

There truly are no words to describe the moments that followed. Nor do I know how long they lasted. But after they had passed our astonished numbness thawed into speech.

'Rose!' screamed Caddy.

'Caddy!' I cried, and I hugged her.

And she was very uncomfortable to hug.

Then we both spoke together in unenchanted voices.

'I don't believe it!' said Caddy. 'You're one of those idiot kids that are mucking about in the grounds!'

While at the same time I said,

'Gross! You've got some awful zoo animal stuffed up your jacket.'

And I turned my torch on her to see what it was and Caddy grabbed it from my hand.

But not quite in time.

Other people were about. We could hear their voices calling and see the flashes of their lights.

They were people in a different world.

It was dark where we were standing. Caddy had turned the torches off. And it was quiet (except for a bit of understandable snuffling).

So I said,

'I suppose that's Buttercup.'

'You must see, Rose,' said Caddy (after much more snuffling), 'that I couldn't call him Buttercup. It would be awful for a boy. Anyway I think it's about time our family went in for a few plain names. I like Carlos myself, and he looks a bit like a Carlos, but that's the Patagonian sea lion's name too, so I don't know. A lot of people here call him Tootles. And don't you dare tell anyone!'

Am I likely to tell anyone that I have a nephew called Tootles? Or insist that he be named Buttercup instead?

And how can I judge whether he looks like a Carlos or not in the dark?

'Oh all right,' said Caddy grudgingly, and turned the torch on him for a moment. 'I didn't mean you weren't to tell anyone he was called Tootles, I meant you weren't to tell anyone about him *at all!* Isn't he gorgeous?'

Yes, he is. He is completely gorgeous. His eyes are shining slits of darkness. His skin is olive brown. His hair is black, and already long enough for Caddy to twist into a ponytail. He will grow up into one of those people who lean back to smile and jump so easily it looks like slow motion and steer cars with their knees and snitch roses from gardens to give to girls and write with their left hand and own two pairs of jeans and one jacket and fall in love from such a height and so hard and so completely that they never quite recover from the drop.

But at least he will have me to look out for him.

In the distance, but coming closer, we could see torchlight. Someone called, 'We've found two of them!' and I heard Molly's voice, very clear and happy, saying, 'I knew it was a tiger!' Caddy hurriedly stuffed Buttercup into a sort of bag thing she had round her neck.

'You go and get found too,' she ordered, hugging me properly this time.

'But I don't want to yet!'

'You must! And absolutely *don't* say a word about Buttercup. (I'm not going to call him that!) Understand? Not to anyone!'

I knew perfectly well who she meant by anyone.

Michael.

I said I didn't see why.

'Because,' said Caddy, 'he's put up with enough. Ever since I gave him back his ring and then nearly married Alex and we had that awful row last year in Portugal that you don't know about.'

'But . . .' I began.

'Poor, poor darling Michael!' continued Caddy. 'I'm giving him his freedom.' (Snuffle, snuffle, snuffle.) 'So promise!'

I'm very, very fond of my nutty big sister, and I know that she's just as fond of me. If our meeting outside the arctic foxes' shed was not quite perfect it was because of nothing other than circumstances beyond our control.

Still, I didn't like it when I had to let go of her and Buttercup and she pushed me away and disappeared into the blackness. Nor when, from that blackness, her voice hissed,

'Don't forget you promised!'

206

*

I didn't promise.

I never knew a day could be so long until that one. And when I finally arrived home (delivered by Kiran's father) I was so tired I was hardly surprised to find Daddy waiting up for me.

He was just one more phenomenon on the way to bed.

Tuesday 19th December

The Stable and the Shed

'I cannot be angry with you,' said the Head to Molly and Kiran and me. 'Nor can I punish you. I can't even tell you off as I should. I am just so thankful to have you safe.'

This was pretty much what our families had said, and we smiled at each other and sighed with relief.

And then the Head gave us such a tremendous, detailed, unrestrained and furious BLASTING that our coordination was affected and we could hardly speak or stagger out of the door and we only got back to our classroom by keeping very silent and holding on to walls.

And I personally felt as if the world had exploded around me and left me standing alone.

Presently Kiran recovered enough to speak and she said, 'I bet that's nothing compared to what he says to Mr Spencer.'

This delicious thought made all three of us instantly one hundred per cent well.

*

The rest of the day at school was unusually nice. Mr Spencer, we were told, was Very Busy Somewhere Else. This meant that Mrs Shah took our register. She did it very carefully, making sure she had seen every person full length and facing forward before she ticked them off. Afterwards she counted us. And she continued to count us at odd intervals all through the day. She said, 'If any more of you disappear it won't be my fault.'

In between countings Mrs Shah helped us to decorate our classroom with leftover Christmas decorations. Then she gave us a large chocolate-filled Advent calendar that she had bought with her own money and we opened the first nineteen doors all in one go. After that she read us a Christmas story. We'd had that story every Christmas since Miss Farley's class, but we did not mind. It is a long time since anybody bothered to read us a story.

In the afternoon we were sent to the hall to help Class 1 rehearse their Nativity play.

I think they need a lot of help.

Mummy's costumes look a bit tatty close up, but they are all right from a distance, and the manger is filled with real hay (and also glitter hearts and stars which I think is a mistake). It is a pity that Baby Jesus is really Baby Annabel and much too girlie looking and pink. I offered to paint her a more Holy colour. I could have done that quite easily and it would have washed off afterwards, but I wasn't allowed. I also think Mary and Joseph need to calm down. When the innkeeper said they would have to sleep in the stable, Joseph said, 'Oh cool, that is amazing,' and Mary punched the air. I'm sure the first Joseph and Mary weren't that thrilled.

Class 1 don't know anything about real life, and I don't suppose any of them have ever seen an actual stable. I tried to explain to Mary and Joseph how uncomfortable it would have been and I should know. I spent a whole evening in an arctic foxes' shed with no bathroom and there cannot be much difference. It was no good though, Mary and Joseph would not listen because Kiran had got to them first. Kiran described the arctic foxes' shed so unnaturally that it sounded like a small dark patch of Heaven. Also she gave Class 1 the bad idea of squeezing in a large feast, similar to the feast we had in the shed, between the birth of Baby Jesus and the arrival of the shepherds.

Class 1 are so messy that half the time the dinner ladies make them eat their lunches wearing paper-towel *bibs!* Mummy's costumes would be ruined. So I said the feast was a terrible idea and they should sing 'Away in a Manger' instead. Their class teacher agreed with me and said the last thing Mary and Joseph needed was a dose of E numbers in the middle of the Nativity; they were overexcited enough as it was.

So I won.

Also, before the end of the afternoon I managed to get all the glitter out of the manger. I hid it in the bin under a box of frankincense that got squashed.

'You're a perfectionist, Rose,' said the Class 1 teacher, watching me.

Yes I am.

I'd only just got rid of the glitter when Mrs Shah came to count us one last time, and to send us home. All day long we hadn't seen or heard Mr Spencer once. Not a snigger. Not a whisker. Not a sweaty footprint.

So.

I had a surprise when I got out of school. Saffron and Sarah were waiting there to take me into town. I was a bit worried about this because Daddy (over my morning porridge) told me that after school I was to come straight home, no chatting, lingering, playing silly games or tiger hunting on the way, and if I didn't, tomorrow he would *come and meet me at the gate.*

No, no, no! Anything but Daddy waiting at the gate, chatting up the Infants' mums.

'He knows we're meeting you,' said Saffy. 'We phoned him. We are going to buy the Christmas tree, so hurry up! And I think you should stop sulking at me, Rose! Do you really think I would have let you down on Saturday on purpose? I couldn't help it. I was having a terrible time! I lost *all my Christmas shopping*!'

Oh, poor Saffy! That is too horrible. I could not bear it if I lost all my Christmas shopping. It is my most precious stuff and I will share it all with Saffron if she likes.

'I am sorry, I am sorry, I am sorry!' I said. 'What will you do?'

'Improvise,' said Saffy, airily.

I always knew Saffron was brave.

All the same, I was careful to choose a rather small tree so that Saffy should not be too worried about what could fill the space underneath. We put it on to Sarah's lap to get it home. Sarah balanced it, while Saffy and I pushed. On the way back we talked so much about Daddy arriving home, and the porridge he insists on making, and where everyone could possibly sleep, that Sarah said we sounded like the three bears.

'The three bears got off easily compared to us,' said Saffron. 'At least Goldilocks' mother did not bunk off to Spain. And Goldilocks didn't turn up with a drum kit either, and none of the bears were scarred for life by falling over it. What do you want for Christmas, Rose? Since I am starting all over again.'

I said the nicest thing would be her back home.

'That is asking a bit much,' said Saffron gloomily. 'I'll do anything for you within reason, Rose, but I'm blowed if I'm sleeping with Goldilocks.'

Our house was very quiet. David and Indigo were out doing Indigo's papers. Mummy was upstairs, with a big notice on her door saying, 'Do Not Disturb' in Daddy's writing. And Daddy

was

in

the

shed

!!!!!!!!

I went to see him. He was just finishing his fourth St Matthew's of the day, jade-green coloured sky (with white lace cloud formations), misty gravestones, the lot.

'It was the only way I could think of to keep your mother in bed,' he said, stretching his arms and cramping and uncramping his fingers. 'Six more to go, I'll knock 'em off in the morning. You can't call it forgery; they're not exactly Art.'

Daddy has more things bad about him, and more things good about him, than anybody else I know.

Then there was supper to be eaten ('I've made a casserole,' said Daddy very smugly) and the tree to be decorated and then we had to decide whether or not we should put our presents underneath. Indigo and I thought we should (I cannot wait to see what my presents look like all piled up there) but Saffy said it wasn't fair because all hers were lost, and David looked so uncomfortable I was sorry for him. It was even worse when Sarah's mother came round to pick up Saffron and Sarah and invited us all for Christmas dinner. David looked absolutely miserable, even when she said very kindly, 'And David too of course, if he's still here. The more the merrier!'

David didn't say anything at all but Daddy put his arm round his shoulders and said, 'Of course he'll still be here!'

'Of course he will,' agreed Mummy, who had come down to see the tree. 'Whatever would we do without him?'

(All very nice polite grown-up stuff.)

Whatever will we do with him though?

David takes up a lot of space.

And so does his drum kit.

Also he's not happy. I know I ought to worry about him, but I haven't had time yet, because all day long, whatever I have been doing, the same thought has been going round and round in my head.

What about Caddy and Buttercup?

Wednesday 20th December

Darling Michael
followed by:
Kiran
and then:
The Hero and the Stony Tower, Dungeon, Cell, Shed

Darling Michael

All yesterday I worried about Caddy and Buttercup. What can I do? I need to talk to Michael, but I don't know how. I don't know where he lives any more, and there are no Michael Cadogens in the telephone book.

'It's easy,' said Kiran. 'Ring the driving school he works for. Their number is painted on all their cars.'

I tried last night, but it didn't work. That number is for booking lessons, the office hours are between eight and five, if you would like us to get back to you please leave a message after the tone. Said a very bossy voice indeed.

Oh.

Well then.

*

'Well, *I* know what *I* would do,' said Kiran when I told her at school. 'Wouldn't you, Mollipop?'

'Yes, I would!' said Molly at once. 'I definitely would!'

'What?' I asked. 'What are you talking about?'

'Which would you like, Rose?' asked Kiran suddenly. 'To know what we're talking about or a lovely surprise?'

A lovely surprise.

So Kiran and Molly went into a happy huddle together, during which something exchanged hands, and then Kiran disappeared behind the Portakabin and Molly kept me out of the way.

Molly is very pleased with herself at the moment on account of her correct identification of the new zoo tiger by its roars in the dark, a very kind letter indeed from the Zoo inviting *our whole class* for a sleepover and night-time expedition as soon as the weather gets warmer, and the continued unexplained absence of Mr Spencer. We had Mrs Shah again today who gave us home-made sums of the reindeer and carrot variety.

'If a reindeer receives 3 carrots at 2000 homes and each carrot weighs 10g and he uses up 20g of carrot energy travelling between each home and 20,000g on the journey back to the North Pole (although none on the journey out because it is all downhill) how much more will he weigh on

Christmas morning?' said Mrs Shah. 'Put your hand down, Kiran dear, and see what you can make of this A-level Maths paper while the others work it out. Rose, if you would like to just draw the reindeer that will be quite all right since it is very nearly Christmas.'

But I said I would have a go and I did although for the first hour or two of my attempt it seemed as if the only way possible would be to draw not only the reindeer but also the two thousand houses and then count out the three carrots at each one on my fingers. Which I was prepared to do and was doing until at house number two hundred and forty-something my brain took a great leap forward like all Santa's reindeer starting off at once and I UNDERSTOOD. A revelation so complete and astonishing I had to go to the bathroom to see if my face had changed to something more like Kiran's (to whom this sort of thing has happened several times a day all her life). But it hadn't. (30g.)

Obvious.

Later we were divided into groups where we made pink, white, and green peppermint creams and decorated boxes to put them in. Each group made a different colour and there were enough for us to have nine each to take home and one to try in class.

Mrs Shah is brilliant. At lunchtime Molly collected

money to buy her a Christmas present from our class and we got enough for a mug saying WORLD'S BEST EVER TEACHER and a chocolate orange and a musical card that plays 'Silent Night' very fast.

Kiran and Molly and I bought them on the way home and then I went off

For

My

Initial Free Driving Lesson.

With Mr Cadogen.

Pick up at number 27 Magnolia Road.

(Which happens to be Sarah's house.)

My lovely surprise, booked by Kiran this morning using Molly's mobile phone and Kiran's most grown-up voice.

And I thought,

It won't work

It won't work

It won't work

GOOD GRIEF!

So I grab open the passenger door, chuck in my school bag and fling myself into the seat before Michael can say, 'Yes right, and what do you think you're playing at, Rose?'

('Keep calm,' Kiran had advised, 'and be *very* tactful.')

'Oh Michael!' I said. 'Oh Michael, I haven't seen you for ages.'

'I knew there was something fishy about that booking,' said Michael. 'Out you get!'

'I've bought you a Christmas present,' I said. 'It's the same as Caddy's, only a different picture so you can think of her when you look at it, and she'll be the same, thinking of you.'

'I'm taking you home,' said Michael. 'Put your seat belt on.'

'No, not yet. I've got to tell you something.'

'Leave it please, Rose,' said Michael, reaching over for my seat belt, strapping me in, starting the engine and pulling away from the kerb. 'There's nothing left to say.'

'Just let me tell you about Buttercup!'

Michael yawned.

'Because she's at the Zoo and I think you ought to know.'

'Poor old Buttercup,' said Michael. 'I am absolutely not getting involved.'

It is a three-minute walk from Sarah's house to ours. That makes it about a one-minute drive. One minute is not long enough to change three futures and any moment I was going to be decanted on to the pavement.

'Now, what's the matter with you?' asked Michael, a bit crossly.

'Oh Michael,' I wailed, abandoning tact and calm which had not been the slightest use anyway. 'What if you've got another girlfriend or something or even got married to someone; oh what will happen to Buttercup and Caddy then . . . would you tell me if you had?'

Michael got out, walked round the car, opened my door and said, 'Yes, Rose. I would tell you if I had.'

And he looked like darling Michael again when he said it. So I jumped out and hugged him very hard and I said, 'She said not to tell you. Oh Michael, I wish Caddy had married you instead of not marrying Alex.'

'So do I,' said Michael, and then he got back into his car and drove away.

But at least now he knows everything.

Or does he?

Kiran

Kiran, calling in to admire our Christmas tree and dragging from me word by word exactly what I had said, was of the opinion that Michael can know nothing at all. Unless he has something called ESP which is hereditary in her family but they don't talk about it because it frightens the non-related (but doomed).

'Is that me?'

'Just don't ask, Rose,' said Kiran and changed the subject by admiring our tree which she thought was easily as good as their Six-Foot Deluxe Fibre-Optic Norwegian Fir.

'Does it pack flat?' she enquired.

'NO!' I yelled at my mathematical-genius-ESP-wielding friend. 'It does not pack flat! It is a tree!'

Crikey!

The Hero and the Stony Tower, Dungeon, Cell, Shed

Daddy has been very useful today. He finished the last six St Matthew's and then rushed all ten of them into town to the picture framer. While the framer was busy Daddy wandered around the marketplace, buying vegetables and organic porridge and Having a Think. And then he took the pictures home again, and after supper he presented them to Mummy in a complete and complacent pile, with a red rose on top.

Mummy, who has been recovering like mad ever since he got home, hugged him.

'I think those pictures were making me ill,' she said.

'And that shed had turned into a dungeon, a hermit's cell, a stony tower. I can't believe I haven't got to go back in there till after Christmas.'

'If I had my way you would never go back in there again,' said Daddy, smugly admiring his perfect perspectives (Daddy has never lost a vanishing point in his life). 'Why don't I chuck the place in town (I miss you all so much and it is not paying for itself as it should) and move Back Up Here?'

What an astonishing idea!

'Back Up Here?' we all repeated, and Indigo added, 'But you hate Up Here! This is the North, remember? Where they sit around on doorsteps and can't say grass?'

For this was the description of our home given by Daddy to a fellow artist some years ago, and Indigo had overheard and passed it on. And also, it seemed, kept it in mind ever since.

David's lips moved, silently mouthing 'Grass. Grass,' until he had reassured himself that he could do it, and Daddy looked very surprised.

'Did I say that?' he asked. 'I apologize. I am ashamed of myself.'

But he recovered from his shame very quickly (as usual) and continued with his astonishing idea.

223

'I was thinking it all out this morning,' he said. 'I could take one of those little shops looking on to the marketplace and Do it Up for Antiques, with a Gallery upstairs, and a Studio at the top. It would be an Enhancement, an Oasis, a place where people come to Refresh a Dream. Before we know it we could be Raking it In. I don't see why it shouldn't be an absolute gold mine if we get the pricing right . . .'

Poor old Daddy! We shouldn't have laughed like we did. He had been absolutely heroic since he came back, sleeping on the sofa, and being kind to David, and not unnecessarily ratty about my evening in the arctic foxes' shed. And he had cooked us supper (risotto with parmesan and toasted almonds) and accomplished ten St Matthew's in less than twenty-four hours, and spent the whole afternoon shifting furniture. Indigo's enormous wardrobe was now on the landing, and a proper bed for David had been installed in its place. So now, as soon as the drum kit was relocated, Saffy could have her room again.

So we shouldn't have laughed.

But we did.

Thursday 21st December

I woke up very early this morning to finish a book called *A Necklace of Raindrops*. Since Monday-at-the-Zoo I have also read most of *The Blue Fairy Book* and *The Tailor of Gloucester* and I have just started another called *The Dream Fighter*.

I read all the time and everywhere; in bed, in the bathroom, cleaning my teeth and eating my breakfast, waiting in the dinner queue at school. I read while David drums and Daddy fills bin bags and Mummy gets better and Saffron shops and Indigo disappears with Sarah. Caddy's bookshelf is wonderful.

Kiran says it's full of fairy stories. If it is, then I like fairy stories. Fairy stories are fair. In them wishes are granted, words are enchanted, the honest and brave make it safely through to the last page and the baddies have to either give up their wickedness for ever and ever, no going back, or get ruthlessly written out of the story, which they hardly ever survive. Also in fairy stories there are hardly any of those half-good half-bad people that crop up so constantly in real life and are so difficult to believe in.

I wonder if Daddy really will stay.

And I wonder if Mr Spencer will be written out of the story.

Another school day and no Mr Spencer. Mrs Shah and the Head are sharing us again. When we ask probing questions about the health of Mr S they say it is none of our business. A rumour started going round that he had won the Lottery and left for good. Mrs Shah and the Head smiled enigmatically and refused to confirm or deny it, so we hunted out Miss Farley, our rather grumpy class teacher from two years ago. She was piling lost property under the entrance-hall Christmas tree and looking very unenigmatic indeed.

'Not one of these items is labelled,' she grumbled. 'Look at it all! Brand new sweatshirts! Jackets! Shoes! Don't parents notice when their kids come home with only one shoe? Pencil cases, a bag of mouldy knobbly things . . .'

'Conkers,' said Molly, reassuringly.

'. . . two skateboards, four crutches, a cat basket . . . What did you say you had lost, Rose?'

'Mr Spencer.'

'Ho!' said Miss Farley, jabbing the heap under the Christmas tree with a lost shrimping net. 'Well, he's not here, I am very sorry to report.'

'Do you think he really has won the Lottery?' asked Kiran.

'*Yes I do!*' said Miss Farley. '*Yes I certainly do!* There is no justice in this world and who handed him the winning ticket? *You* three!'

'No we didn't!'

'What were you thinking of?' continued Miss Farley. 'Didn't you realize the consequences to a teacher of losing three pupils on a school trip? And I hear he spent the entire time sitting smoking in the warm and drinking rum and coffee. Not to mention the tiny mistake of handing the register to a minor who got bored with taking care of it and *threw it away?*'

'Did Kai . . . ?'

'It was bagged up with all the zoo rubbish on Monday night,' said Miss Farley. 'And it took half of Tuesday, searching through goodness-knows-what-but-I-don't-suppose-it-was-very-fragrant to find it again. The wretched man is signed off indefinitely with stress . . .'

'*How long is indefinitely?*'

'You may well ask! And on full pay . . .'

'*Full pay!*'

'Therefore that being the case the first thing he did was book a flight to the Caribbean . . .'

'Not truly?'

'He is probably there right now under a palm tree which

227

is a slightly better prospect than anything in sight for *me* this Christmas.'

Oh.

'There must be *some* disadvantages,' said Kiran, at last.

'Only utter disgrace,' said Miss Farley, handing us each a chocolate angel and choosing one for herself. 'And let's face it, he won't care a bit.'

Then she bit off her angel's head and cheered up.

'Still, there may be a hurricane. Or jellyfish. Or land crabs. I've heard that one falling coconut can lay you out flat!'

'Yes, I'm sure it could,' agreed Molly comfortingly.

'Personally I wouldn't say thank you for the Caribbean at Christmas!' said Miss Farley (cheering up very rapidly as the chocolate molecules soaked into her brain). 'It's not traditional, for one thing.'

Then she gobbled up the rest of her angel and shooed us outside.

'Miss Farley is the best teacher in the school,' said Kiran. 'You can learn more in five minutes with her than you can in a week with any of the others.'

The Mr Spencer news was fascinating. Kiran, Molly and I walked home together talking about hurricanes and things with such concentration that we didn't notice anything unusual until Kiran asked, 'Did you book another driving lesson, Rose?'

And there was Michael.

'It has taken me twenty-four hours to work out what you were talking about yesterday,' he said. 'Have you still got that ring, Rosy Pose?'

'What ring?' asked Molly and Kiran, but I knew what ring. The beautiful platinum and diamond one that he bought for Caddy nearly three years before and had later given to me for safe keeping.

'Of course I have still got it,' I said. 'Wait and I will bring it. I have put it away in a very safe place.'

There are many very safe places in my bedroom, and with Molly and Kiran's help I searched them all. I found a bundle of dead roses, a home-made CD from America, several guitar picks (how I wish I could see Tom again), a photo of me on Grandad's knee, a sponge shaped like a dinosaur, a T-shirt with the sleeves chopped off and CRIME PAYS in iron-on letters across the front, a hat which I had when I was five and which was exactly like a hat that Sarah used to wear, a packet of banana-flavoured chews (why did I keep them?) and a picture of our house that I drew long, long ago on my first day at school. And it is very funny because Mummy's shed is there, all rainbow-coloured, and the garden streams away from the roof like a banner in the wind. And I found, last of all, in the pocket of a jacket that used to be Indigo's, the diamond ring.

'Wish me luck,' said Michael as he drove away.

'Good luck! Good luck!' shrieked Molly and Kiran. 'Tell us what happens! Hurry back soon! Listen out for the tiger! Rose says nobody could not love Buttercup!'

And when he had gone they said, 'Oh, I wonder what will happen! I wonder if it will be all right!'

You would think that neither of them had ever read a book in their lives.

All This Was Meant To Be

'Your house seems different,' remarked Kiran when she called for me this morning.

'What sort of different?'

'Bigger,' said Kiran.

She's right, the house does seem bigger. It has been growing ever since Daddy came home.

Daddy keeps having mini-conferences. They go like this:

'While I have got you all together,' says Daddy, leaning against the living-room door so we are trapped, 'I would just like a quick opinion on the optimum number of vacuum cleaners necessary in a house this size. Eve?'

'Darling, I understand what you are saying,' says Mummy, who is now well enough to arrange ivy leaves very carefully round the fireplace. 'They disappear, I know they do. But there must be one somewhere about because it really doesn't seem that long since I bought the last. . .'

'It was when Rose's beanbag popped,' said Indigo.

'Popped, or was snipped open to see what was inside?'

asked Saffron. 'Why've you got the angel down off the tree, Rose?'

'I'm making her some proper knickers.'

'Tighten up her wings then, while you've got her down.'

'How's she going to fly with tight wings?' asked Indigo.

'Did she fly before, then?' asked Sarah. 'Without proper knickers?'

'Two,' said David. 'Vacuum cleaners,' he added, seeing everyone except Daddy looking completely baffled. 'One for upstairs and one for downstairs. And if one went wrong you'd have a spare.'

'I don't think anyone could disagree with that, David,' says Daddy warmly. 'Eve?'

'Two would probably be perfect,' agreed Mummy, gilding ivy berries with a tiny paintbrush dipped in gold.

'Not eight, then?' asks Daddy.

Eight.

Daddy has done it again. Eight is the number of vacuum cleaners he has found, and we cannot hide our surprise, even though he has already confronted us with eleven sleeping bags, five sets of Christmas lights, too many steam irons and hairdryers to contemplate, and several similar shameful accumulations. Our habit of dealing with malfunctioning, inadequate, or just plain lost items by rushing to the shops has been exposed, as Saffron says, in all its profligate disgracefulness.

But where did all the zip-up fleeces come from?

And two bin bags of wellington boots?

'We may never know,' says Daddy.

The charity shops are being restocked at a tremendous rate.

David has been very useful to Daddy in his excavating and redistributing activities. A strange sort of friendship has grown between them. I think this is partly because David takes Daddy seriously, and partly because Daddy understands what David is up against.

Daddy found out what David was up against the evening he telephoned David's mother on her mobile for a Quiet Word.

I think he picked a bad moment. David's mother was not having anything like as good a time in sunny Spain as she had expected, and yet was trapped in the place for another week and a half. I don't know exactly what she said to Daddy when he started to explain his theories on Successful Family Life, but I don't think she was polite.

Daddy was very nice to David afterwards. He fixed him up a bedside lamp and asked for a drumming demonstration and had a go himself and behaved so well that we were proud of him, even when he offered rubbish drumming advice. And Mummy said to Sarah's mother on the phone, 'We are counting on having David for Christmas at least, and we hope for New Year too,' and she made sure David overheard when she said it.

We're doing our best.

I am going to give him the peppermint creams I made at school for Christmas. I nearly ate them, and then I thought of it. I've made them a new box painted to look like a drum. Kiran was a bit unencouraging about it though.

'I hope he gets more than peppermint creams for Christmas,' she said. 'Peppermint creams isn't much.'

How true.

I stopped right there in the middle of the street and borrowed Kiran's mobile phone and texted Saffy and Indigo and Sarah saying:

v v urgent 4 u 2 by xmas present dvd not pppmt crms lv rose

After that I rang home and explained the same thing to Mummy and she said, 'What David needs is Love, Rosy Pose, but I will pass on your message to Father Christmas next time we have a chat.'

So I asked to speak to Daddy and he said, 'I'm on to it, Rose.'

'I wish I could boss my parents around like that,' said Kiran enviously. 'I can't even make mine use eco-friendly washing powder.'

'Buy them some for Christmas,' I said. 'Then they'll have no choice.'

Buying eco-friendly washing powder for Kiran's parents' Christmas made us very late for school. Mrs Shah was waiting for us in the entrance hall brandishing the register and saying, 'One more minute and I was going to ring your families. Where have you been?'

'Only buying eco-friendly washing powder for my parents' Christmas,' said Kiran soothingly. 'Then they will have a present each to unwrap because I have already got them a solar-powered doorbell which requires minimal fitting. I am turning them green.'

'You are turning me grey,' said Mrs Shah, crossly. 'I shall be glad when All This Performance Is Over. Anything loses its novelty after two thousand repetitions. Off you go into the hall and try not to be silly.'

I think Mrs Shah is a bit stressed.

Tonight is the school Nativity play performed by Class 1 with an awful lot of help from the rest of the world because Class 1 can do nothing unaided. Mary and Joseph are the worst of the lot. If the real Mary and Joseph were anything like our Mary and Joseph there would be no Christmas because Christianity would have got no further than a big fight over who got the donkey somewhere along the road to Bethlehem.

This Friday morning was the dress rehearsal. That meant assembling on stage the angels, the shepherds, the inn-door-that-really-opens, the stable and the star and the manger (glitter-free), Mary and Joseph and the much fought over two-dimensional cardboard donkey.

And, of course, Baby Jesus.

In our school version of the Christmas story Baby Jesus makes his first appearance when he is passed (fully dressed and fast asleep) by the angel Gabriel into the eager grabby little hands of Mary. (Who is forced to let go of the donkey at last and for ever – the donkey at once being seized by Joseph with an unholy cry of 'Miss said now I could keep him till the end'.)

But what has happened to Baby Jesus?

Baby Jesus is no longer pink and girlie. He is a beautiful brown. I suppose this is slightly my fault for suggesting we paint him, but it is much more Kai's for doing it. Yesterday Kai covered Baby Jesus (who used to be Baby Annabel) with Golden Oak wood preservative and today he is sticking to everything. Gabriel has brown gluey patches all down his front, and Mary had a terrible job laying him in the manger because he stuck to her hands. And now he looks more like a porcupine than a baby because he is bristling with hay.

You'd have thought the Class 1 teacher would go mad, but she didn't. She has taught Class 1 for years and is therefore immune to disaster and hardened to calamity.

'Who can supply a new Baby Jesus in time for tonight?' she asked, not a bit flustered.

Then there was a sound like excited chickens as Class 1 all offered at once to supply the manger with Action Man, Barbie, an immense variety of dinosaurs and several varieties of fake human babies with unhygienic battery-powered abilities and very loud voices.

'We don't want anything like that,' said Class 1's teacher firmly. 'We want a nice quiet Baby Jesus with no added burps, guns, disco moves, horns, scales, lasers or wind-out multicoloured grow 'n' style hair. Molly, do you think you . . .'

But I, whose thoughts had been filled for hours with Caddy and Michael and most of all Buttercup, said, 'Oh let me, let me, let me, let me!'

'Why?' asked Molly and Kiran in surprise.

Because I have a feeling.

A sudden wonderful feeling.

That

All this was meant to be.

Saturday 23rd December

Once in Every Generation

David's drum kit is now in the shed. He and Indigo put it there last night when we got home from the superb best ever end of term Nativity play.

I crept past Saffy's door and downstairs very early today. Last night when Michael drove away he'd called, 'Back in the morning!'

I didn't want him arriving and finding no one awake, but I needn't have worried. Daddy was already in the kitchen. He was twisting about in front of the mirror trying to see the top of his head. The bald bit.

'You can hardly notice,' I told him, to comfort him.

'Notice what?'

'The bald bit.'

'Thank you, Rose,' said Daddy sadly.

Then we helped each other make some tea and I had a banana and Daddy didn't and it was very quiet except for the clock, ticking once a second, to prove it was still there. Daddy sighed.

'Rose,' he said. 'I feel suddenly old. I didn't realize how the years had gone by. Don't try to look sympathetic because you cannot possibly understand.'

Yes I can. I have just spent a week with Class 1 and they are like people from another planet but really they are just me, five years ago. Indigo and Saffy and Sarah and Caddy have changed too. They are turning into the sort of people I used to call Grown Up and I can't stop them, although I would if I could. I would slow them down anyway. Sometimes I want to shout, 'Wait for me! Wait for me!'

Like I did when I was little and they walked too fast.

They always turned back then, however much of a hurry they were in, but I don't think they can turn back now.

So I do understand.

While I was trying to think of a way of telling Daddy how clearly I comprehended the relentless sweeping of the years through time he was on the telephone booking a year's membership of the gym. He booked Platinum Level. Very expensive indeed because it includes the pool and the squash courts and the sauna and the sun rooms as well as unlimited access to all the treadmills and rowing machines and bikes that don't go anywhere.

Spending so much money cheered Daddy up.

'After all,' he said, gently patting the place on his head that had been worrying him so much, 'you are only as old as you feel.'

Poor Daddy. But he got the biggest surprise of anyone yesterday, because he was Christmas shopping all afternoon (as ordered by me) and he went straight from town to school for the Nativity play. And he walked in a cool snappy shopper laden with beanies and band T-shirts and earrings and cashmere and was instantly transformed into Baby Jesus's Grandad.

Buttercup was a perfect Baby Jesus. Caddy (hastily dressed as an extra angel and hovering at the side of the stage) needn't have been there at all. I think he may grow up to be a very talented actor because although it was quite a simple thing he had to do, just lie nicely on some hay, he managed it very well indeed. Class 1 had just as simple things to do, but they didn't manage them half as well. The Wise Men had to be asked in front of everyone to settle down and leave the presents alone. And we'll need a new donkey next year. With stronger ears.

None of that really mattered though. The only truly important thing was that it was nearly Christmas, and

Buttercup had arrived in time to be Baby Jesus. He was there when I got home and I had no problem persuading Caddy to lend him to me.

'He is used to being worshipped,' she said, and in no time at all we were all rushing back to school together, Mummy and Caddy and Michael and Saffy and Sarah and David and Indigo, too. All of us except Daddy, who we completely forgot. He arrived a little late, when everyone was sitting down, and the recorders were taking enormous breaths, about to start the Overture.

Miss Farley recognized him.

'We must find you a seat near the front!' she cried, loud enough for the whole school to hear and abandoning her raffle tickets in her excitement. 'Recorders! One moment please while we find a place for Baby Jesus's grandad!'

'I beg—' began Daddy, but what he begged was never heard because the recorder players found they could hold their breaths no longer and the 'Sans Day Carol' erupted almost simultaneously from both sides of the stage.

I turned round to smile at Daddy and he looked like he had been hit on the head with something hard.

Although so did quite a lot of the audience so perhaps it was only the music.

*

242

'In the New Year,' said Daddy, measuring out oats for porridge and bouncing a little on the balls of his feet because he was now a Platinum Level gym member, 'I shall go for a jog every morning.'

'What, outside?' I asked, astonished.

'Yes, of course outside,' said Daddy.

'Maybe you have not seen outside lately,' I suggested, and I switched the kitchen lights off so that the windows were no longer full of reflections and Daddy could get a good look at the midwinter grimness of our orange-lit, black-puddled, car-splashy street.

'Well, maybe not every morning,' he said. 'Stop laughing like that, you'll disturb the whole house. There is one rule you might as well learn about living with babies, Rose, and it's that you must never ever ever under any circumstances wake them up.'

'Why not?'

'I don't know,' admitted Daddy. 'I never worked it out. But it's true. You wait and see.'

(I am rather worried. I hope Daddy likes Buttercup. He was so quiet last night that I got Indigo outside to whisper.

'It is only shock,' said Indigo, who had laughed himself double at Daddy's face.)

'It's a whole new world,' said Daddy. 'Start living on

243

tiptoe. Who did you think he looked like then, Rose?'

What! Did Daddy not even glance at his grandson last night? Were the exclamations not loud enough? Was Michael's smirk not wide enough? Were the lights not bright enough? How could Daddy possibly not have noticed what I had seen by shaky torchlight in an arctic foxes' den?

'Of course, superficially, he is very like Michael,' said Daddy. 'But his hands, I looked particularly at his hands, his hands are exactly like mine! Once in every generation. You've got them too.'

Oh.

I looked at Daddy's clean brown hands, with the gold ring and the little finger ring and the smooth bones at the knuckles and I looked at mine, still scratched from brambles, not very washed looking, pinkish grey and rough on the backs, and I thought of Buttercup's which were very like Baby Annabel's.

'You see,' said Daddy smugly.

Indigo was quite right. I need not have worried.

'Yes,' I said. 'I do see.'

Christmas shopping again today. Daddy has very kindly given me three months' pocket money in advance and Molly and Kiran are coming to help me. We have reluctantly

244

decided against gold, frankincense, myrrh and live sheep. Saffy and Sarah have been looking at the labels in his clothes to see what size he is. Obviously they will be buying him something to wear. But when Michael arrived for breakfast this morning I asked him very privately (because of course by now he's seen Caddy's flat at the Zoo) if he'd noticed whether Buttercup owned a teddy bear.

'It is a weird thing, Rose,' said Michael, looking at me with thoughtful half-shut gleaming eyes, 'but I don't think he does.'

How lovely to have a day when the only thing you have to worry about is where to find the World's Best Ever Teddy Bear.

Christmas Eve

There are so many presents under our Christmas tree that Saffron has put hers under Sarah's to even it up a bit. I have checked both heaps to make sure David will be OK.

'Saffy has bought him musical socks,' said Sarah, as she helped me check the pile under her tree. 'And I chose a lovely magician's hat from which it is possible to extract a rabbit and a lot of hankies and a large bunch of flowers so that is two good presents. Dad has bought him a miniature remote control car (he is giving everyone remote controlled cars or big pink scarves this year) and Mum has got him a goat in India (because we are all getting goats in India) and a spongebag. I trust that will suffice.'

I said it would suffice brilliantly and Mummy had found him a stocking, and one for Sarah too, and she and Saffron were to hang theirs up at our house and then rush over in the morning to open them.

'I've never had a stocking,' said Sarah. 'When I was little it was always a sack and since then it has been a Vast Heap.

Thank goodness the goats are in India. Have you worked out what Tom's getting for Christmas yet?'

I shook my head.

'Oh, Rose!' said Sarah, laughing.

'Do you know?' I asked. 'Does everyone know except me?'

'I think so, Rosy Pose,' said Sarah.

'When it's Christmas morning here,' I said, 'it will still be Christmas Eve in New York.'

'Christmas Eve is my favourite,' said Sarah.

It's my favourite too.

Monday 25th December

What I Didn't Guess

We spent Christmas morning at our house, and the afternoon at Sarah's. The unwrapping was great fun.

Indigo said, 'Who bought me an ice axe? I've wanted an ice axe for years and years!'

'Me, of course,' said Sarah.

David bought Mummy a miniature rose in a silver pot. It had dark glossy leaves and bright pink flowers just opening out and it smelled like springtime.

'Thank you, thank you, thank you,' said Mummy. 'It is absolutely perfect! Oh Saffy, there's your angel!'

She was standing where she always stands, smiling over the presents at the bottom of the tree.

'I brought her back last night,' said Saffy. 'Rose reminded me.'

Saffy gave me a wonderful shoe box.

David's mother rang up all the way from Spain. She said, 'I hope you are having a lovely day, David, and I am bringing your present home with me.'

'I've got yours here,' said David. 'Do you want to know what it is?'

But she didn't want to know, and she didn't stay to chat.

'Go to Uncle David,' said Caddy, and dumped Buttercup on his knee.

David bounced Buttercup very gently and chanted,

'A rosy apple a penny and a pear.

A bunch of roses she shall wear . . .

(My grandad used to tell me this)

A lily-white horse beside her side

She's the one to be your bride.'

'That reminds me,' said Michael. 'Rose, would you have any objections if Caddy and I got married because we would rather you said so now than at the appropriate point in the service?'

Great shrieks and huggings and tears and laughter.

'I couldn't be more delighted,' said Daddy. 'But this time I'm taking out insurance. Assuming you're inviting Rose, it's only common sense.'

'It's nearly eleven,' said Sarah, suddenly. 'Listen!'

'Why?'

'I thought I heard . . . Saffy?'

Saffy jumped up and glanced out of the window and

then she looked at me with her eyebrows raised and a very peculiar expression on her face.

Mummy took Buttercup off me, although it wasn't her turn.

Daddy sleeked back his hair and the doorbell rang.

'Answer the door, Rose,' said Indigo.

'I will,' said David kindly, and began getting to his feet and Saffy and Sarah and Caddy and Indigo and Michael all grabbed him, exclaiming 'No, you won't!'

So I answered the door.

How can it be?

How can it be that this person is here?

Is it a trick?

Is it Christmas magic?

That guitar strap looks exactly like the one I bought.

'TOM!!!' I screamed, and dragged him in through the door.

Tom said, 'Happy Christmas, Permanent Rose! I can't believe you didn't guess!'

I said, 'But what time is it in New York?'

'What does it matter what time it is in New York?' asked Tom. 'I'm not in New York. I'm here.'

Tuesday 26th December

So What Did You Get For Christmas?

It's turning into a very nice Christmas indeed. Tom and Indigo and David have made a band in the shed and I am the roadie who does all the work. Tom will be here for two weeks. He's staying with his whole family at their witchy grandma's house, the place where I once lost Caddy's diamond and platinum ring.

'Oh that place,' said Kiran when I told her. 'I am afraid it is haunted but Americans probably won't mind.'

'Haunted?' I asked (because we are all going to a party there tomorrow). 'Who by?'

'I *think* some kind of yeti,' said Kiran. 'My brother saw it with his own eyes. It was human-shaped but enormous, and it was out under those big black cedar trees digging a grave in a thunderstorm. So what did you get for Christmas? I got a flute which I definitely didn't ask for.'

I got a mobile phone. It was the last thing in my stocking (apple, peppermints, seahorse-shaped bubble baths, chocolate money, pencils with my name on and my own mobile phone AT LAST!).

'Eve!' said Daddy, a bit shocked, when he saw it.

'She has wanted one for ages,' said Mummy. 'Haven't you, Rose?'

Whatever she says about Father Christmas doing the stockings I think he gets a good deal of help. My mobile must have cost at least two St Matthews, with jade-green skies. I am glad I got her that mug. It's true.

The last thing in David's stocking (apple, peppermints, lime and lemon shower gel, chocolate money and a CD – *Rogue Traders: Here Come the Drums*) was a battered old key to our back door.

'Just so you know you're always welcome,' said Mummy.

Tom

Those cedar trees are certainly creepy but I didn't see the grave-digging Yeti and I didn't like to ask about it because it was Buttercup's first party and it would have been a shame to frighten him. You have to be very careful with babies because you never know how much they can understand.

'He can understand everything,' said Caddy. 'Can't you, Buttercup, darling? We've *got* to stop calling him that!'

So for a little while everyone makes a big effort to call him by his real name. Carlos. Carlos Michael, in fact (Carlos being, by strange coincidence, Michael's second name, as well as the Patagonian sea lion's).

But we are soon back to Buttercup again.

'You should stick it on for real,' said Tom, lying flat on the floor with his guitar across his chest. 'Then me and Indigo and Uncle Davy could play the

Buttercup

Carlos

253

Michael

Cadogen

Blues.'

It is brilliant having a phone that takes pictures. I have taken a million of Tom already.

A moment later he jumped up and passed his guitar to Indigo and said, 'Time for another juggling lesson, Rose!'

Juggling balls were one of my Christmas presents from Tom. It is something he is very good at himself. He says he practises in boring classes at school.

'Then what happens?' asked Indigo.

'Then I get sent out,' said Tom, 'which is great because there's much more space in the corridors.'

When I am away from Tom I worry that he'll change, but when he is within reach I know that we're stuck with him the way he is.

Good.

Thursday 28th December

Frances

I have been reading to Tom's little sister Frances which takes ages because she is three and won't turn over until she has looked at every single inch of the pictures. And she argues all the time, even about the title.

'This book,' I said, 'is called *I WILL NEVER NOT EVER EAT A TOMATO*.'

'To-may-to,' said Frances.

'OK, *I WILL NEVER NOT EVER EAT A TOMATO OR*

A TO-MAY-TO.'

'Why?'

'It says inside the book.'

So Frances grabs the book and lies all over it saying, 'Look at her dress! Look at her eyes! Who is that?'

'That's the girl in the story's big brother.'

'Where's his guitar?' says Frances. 'Read it then!'

'How can I read it when you're lying on the writing?' I ask, so Frances shuts her eyes.

'When she shuts her eyes,' explains Tom, 'she goes invisible. This is useful because you can see right through her.'

Then he read the whole page right through Frances, and took a handful of chocolate money out of one of her ears.

'It wasn't there!' said Frances crossly.

Tom shrugged. 'More where that came from.'

Frances felt her ears, staring at him suspiciously all the while, ordered 'Don't turn over, Rose!' and marched off to find a mirror.

'How did you do it?' I hissed.

'I had them in my sleeve.'

'No. Read through her. Tell me how you read through her so I can do it to Buttercup.'

Tom looked at me in utter astonishment and then asked very patiently, 'Did you really not see that she went slightly transparent when she closed her eyes?'

'*No!*'

'You can only do it with quite large print . . . And it depends what they're wearing, it's easier in summer . . . less clothes . . . Of course, if they cheat and don't close their eyes properly it's impossible. Then you have to bluff and recite it from memory . . . Obviously . . . Are you following, Permanent Rose?'

'Yes, yes.'

'It should be easier with Buttercup. Frances is nearly too big . . . Quite thick bones . . . What are you trying to do?'

I had been trying it secretly with my own hand.

'You need your eyes shut!' said Tom. 'How you gonna get see-through with your eyes wide open?'

'It's a trick,' said Frances, stomping back in.

Is it?

Is it?

Tom's right eyebrow was higher than his left, but his head was bent over his guitar so I could not see the rest of his face. He was playing chords in bits and pieces and he was singing:

'How you gonna get see-through with your eyes wide open?

When you came to New York

You were

My favourite person in New York.'

'That's a nice song,' said Frances.

Uncle Davy

If we want to cheer up David we call him Uncle Davy.

His mother telephoned twice today. The first time she said he had better come home and try again when she got back. The second time she said that he needn't think it would be Open House for every Tom, Dick and Harry and she wasn't taking on That Drum Kit.

Me and Indigo and Mummy dragged this out of him.

Then Indigo went out of the room and had a talk with Daddy and after a while Mummy joined them while I kept David out of the way.

'The more the merrier,' I heard Mummy say when I slipped out to see how they were getting on. 'Isn't that right, Rosy Pose?'

I thought of this house a month ago, when I felt like the only person home.

Yes it is.

*

So after lunch Daddy announced that he was fed up with sitting around doing nothing and he was clearing out the attic and would need everyone to help. Except Mummy because the dust would be bad for her chest, and Buttercup because he would be more use entertaining Mummy.

Seventeen years' worth of accumulated junk was shifted in two hours. Michael piled black bin bags of loot in the doorways of all the closed charity shops in town and made two trips to the tip.

And suddenly we could see Space.

Where there never was space before.

'The window is tiny,' said Mummy, coming up to look.

'Wouldn't be a big job to get a bigger one put in. The floor is fantastic. We can polish it up when they've painted the walls.'

The stairs up to our attic open out of a door on the landing that looks like a cupboard. They're very steep. When Sarah came round to see where everyone had got to we all looked at her rather doubtfully. Except Indigo who hoisted her up and gave her a paintbrush.

Then we painted the whole attic, including the ceiling bits between the beams, Scrubbable Magnolia. We have cans and cans of Scrubbable Magnolia stored in the shed because Daddy buys it in bulk in order to have plenty by when he wants to suddenly eradicate my art.

It took ages and when we were finished Saffy and Sarah and Caddy and I were so exhausted that we hardly had the strength to force the boys to clean the floor. But we did and while they were doing it Sarah's mother came round and when she heard what we were doing she said she had two very nice blue rugs and a futon which no one ever used that she could send round whenever.

And a little plug-in heater.

A desk.

And a chair.

Whenever.

'Now would be good,' said Sarah.

It is not an attic any longer. It is a nice warm wooden-floored blue and cream room.

'You'll have to be really careful of Buttercup on those stairs,' remarked David to Caddy when at last we crawled down for supper.

'Oh,' we all said. 'Oh no! Caddy will be going back to the Zoo as soon as the holiday is over. She has a little flat there that will do until she and Michael decide exactly where they want to be. Saffy can have her room back then.'

'Darling David,' said Mum, 'the attic will just be an

extra room for very welcome people to use whenever they need.'

'That'll be nice for them,' said David sadly, and then he must have seen the way we were all looking at him, and quite suddenly he dropped his head into his arms. And when he lifted it up again, he was shining with one of his great moon-faced smiles.

'I like attics,' he said.

Saturday 30th December

Molly called to say 'I am having a New Year sleepover tomorrow with Kiran and you if you want to come but it must be very exciting at your house so I will completely understand if you don't.'

Of course I want to come.

Sunday 31st December

What I Intend to Do

Since it was New Year's Eve, said Molly, we should make our resolutions for next year because it is very important and how she managed to pass Grade 4 Ballet and stop sucking her thumb.

'It really works,' she said. 'If you keep it up all year.'

'It is how I got my ears pierced,' agreed Kiran. 'I resolved to ask about it reasonably twice a day. I didn't even have to keep it up all year either. Only till around October when they completely cracked and gave in.'

Goodness, these hard-working people! But I'm all right because I don't suck my thumb or take ballet lessons and I already have as many pierced ears as I need (one). In fact, I can think of no improvements I would like to make to the way I am, and Molly, after some thought, said very nicely that neither could she.

'You could resolve to start wearing your glasses every day,' suggested Kiran. 'Instead of only when you want to look at stars.'

No thank you!

Why is it so difficult for everyone to understand distant objects, like street lights and full-length reflections and even Christmas trees and relations, look much, much nicer if they are very slightly blurred?

Not to mention the things like tigers and Mr Spencer that are only bearable at all out of focus.

'Oh,' said Molly. 'Oh yes, I see what you mean! About Mr Spencer anyway. He would be much better blurred. When you look at him, Rose, can you see his moustache?'

'Oh yes.'

'Can you see the things *in* his moustache?'

What!

I am definitely keeping my glasses just for stars!

Then Molly told us her New Year Resolutions. They are:

1. To learn to find her way by the stars like she can by the sun.

('Really?' asked Kiran and me. 'Can you really do that, Mollipop?' 'Only fairly roughly,' said Molly.)

2. To learn to make fire with a fire bow. And without matches.

'Or a flint and steel, of course,' added Molly, 'because that's too easy.'

'How about a magnifying glass?' asked Kiran, trying not

to show that she is nearly out of her depth in this astonishing conversation.

'*Much* too easy,' said Molly. 'And cheating, because where would you find a magnifying glass in the actual wild?'

'Unless you could grind one out of rock crystal,' suggested Kiran (determined not to drown).

'It wouldn't be quick,' said Molly.

'Or ice?'

'Yes, that's a very good idea. I'll try ice,' said Molly. 'And my other things are to learn French because we are going camping in France this summer and to pass Grade 4 Recorder and Grade 5 Ballet.'

'Is that all?' asked Kiran sarcastically.

'Yes but I've got one left from last January to cut off my plaits,' said Molly, cutting off her plaits.

'MOLLY!' shouted Kiran. 'I thought you were supposed to be boring!'

Kiran is going to be busy too. Her New Year Resolution is to humanize Mr Spencer.

'Because whether you see him blurry, or whether you see him plain as plain, he will probably come back and we'll be stuck with him,' she said. 'Stress doesn't last for ever and I should think Caribbean holidays are a pretty good cure. We must not count on hurricanes, or very rich film stars falling in love with him and whisking him away to Hollywood. In fact it is quite unlikely. I intend to humanize him by kindness beginning with a Get Well Card from us all. I bought one and I've started it already and I met Kai in the street so he's signed it too. Everyone's got to either write something nice or a joke.'

'Something nice?' asked Molly in a rather frightened voice.

'Or a joke,' said Kiran firmly. 'Do you like the picture? It's to remind him of the Zoo.'

It was a picture of a poorly parrot in bed.

'It's lovely,' said Molly looking at it admiringly, and then she opened the card up and wrote inside (very carefully, in her best writing and with tiny smiley faces instead of dots on the 'i's).

It was the best school trip ever thank you very much I hope you get well soon I think it is the right time of year to see loggerhead turtles and I hope you do from Molly.

'That's very nice,' said Kiran approvingly. She herself had written:

My brother says that since December 21st daylight is returning to the United Kingdom at a rate of approx 2 minutes a day.

'Your turn, Rose,' said Kiran.

266

I took the card and looked at it. Kai (under an unguessable amount of pressure) had written in very big letters:

Come back soon Mr Spencer, and save us from Class 1.

So I wrote underneath, in even bigger letters:

Come back soon Mr Spencer, and save us from Kiran.

'Not very nice and not very funny,' said Kiran, but I said it was the best I could do and it was nearly midnight and weren't we going to get up and watch the fireworks.

So we did, and had pretend champagne afterwards with Molly's parents, and texted our parents and Caddy and Michael and Indigo and Sarah and Saffron and Tom and Kai and everyone else we knew with mobile phones saying Happy New Year and suddenly it was nearly two o'clock and we were exhausted.

'I forgot,' said Molly sleepily, as we crawled into bed. 'My last resolution. I'm going to write to David Attenborough and tell him about the tiger. Stop laughing, Rose, you ought to write to him too!'

'Me!'

'If it hadn't been for David Attenborough we wouldn't have gone to the Zoo,' said Molly. 'And you wouldn't have found Caddy for Michael and Mr Spencer wouldn't have gone off with stress and we wouldn't have had to help Class 1 with their play, and Kai wouldn't have painted Annabel and so Buttercup couldn't have been Baby Jesus. You know you loved it when Buttercup was Baby Jesus. You said it was just right!'

So I did, and it was. It was perfect. It was a happy ending. Just like in a book.

I have read quite a lot of books lately, and I intend to read many more. And in books I have discovered that there are sometimes lonely patches

And scary times

Disasters

Catastrophes

And long paragraphs of no use at all except possibly (says Saffron) to build up your stamina.

But also there are jokes

Friends

Adventures

And homes.

And these things

Will help you through the long paragraphs

Lonely patches

Perils

And even problems with as many heads as dragons.

To live Happily Ever After.

Which is exactly
What I
Intend
To Do
Forever
Rose.

About the Author

Hilary McKay won the Costa Children's Book Award for *The Skylarks' War*, the *Guardian* Fiction Prize for *The Exiles*, and the Smarties and the Whitbread Award for *The Exiles in Love* and *Saffy's Angel* respectively. She is also the author of *Straw Into Gold*, *A Time of Green Magic* and *The Swallows' Flight*, a companion novel to *The Skylarks' War*, among many critically-acclaimed titles. Hilary studied Botany and Zoology at the University of St Andrews, and worked as a biochemist before the draw of the pen became too strong and she decided to become a full-time writer. Hilary lives in Derbyshire with her family.

*Turn the page for an extract from
the prequel in the series:*

CADDY'S WORLD

Chapter One

Charmed Circle

These were the four girls who were best friends:
    Alison . . . hates everyone.
Ruby is clever.
Beth is perfect.
Caddy, the bravest of the brave.
('Mostly because of spiders,' said Caddy.)

Alison, Ruby, Beth and Caddy had started school together aged four and five, plonked down at the four corners of a blue-topped table in Primary 1 on the first day.

'You four will be friends,' the teacher had told them, pronouncing the words like a charm. She was an elderly person, tall, with silver-streaked hair twirled and looped about her head, black beads, and, remembered Caddy, years afterwards, a sort of purple haze about her that may or may not have been a cardigan.

She was probably a witch.

'You four will be friends,' she said again, and her glance

included all of them: Alison, who was sulking, Ruby with her thumb perilously close to her mouth, and hair cut short like a boy's, and Beth, who was not only perfect, but also dressed utterly and completely in brand new clothes, snow-white underneath, school uniform on top. Last of all Caddy, who had arrived very late because her mother had forgotten the date.

The teacher smiled down from her looped and beaded heights at the table of little girls. Charmed, they smiled back up into the ancient purple haze. Alison, Ruby, Beth and Caddy: bewitched.

They stayed that way. All through primary school and into secondary school. At twelve years old they were still good friends.

'Best friends,' said Caddy.

Alison lived next door to Caddy, in an immaculate house. No visiting went on between the families. Alison's mother used to look out of the window at Caddy's mother, and shake her head and say, 'I'm not getting involved.'

'Absolutely not,' Alison's father would agree.

They were both estate agents. Sometimes Alison's father would gaze at the state of the Cassons' roof and murmur, 'I hope we never have that property on our books. You'd have to be honest.'

2

Their daughter was honest naturally. Alison's was a lovely but insulting honesty that conceded to no one. Her bedroom window faced Caddy's but usually she kept the curtains closed. 'I like my private life,' she told Caddy. All the same she was a helpful friend. When Caddy showed signs of oversleeping on school days she had several times flung slippers and hard-nosed teddy bears at her window and screeched, 'Get up!'

'You could work out a much better system than that,' said Ruby. 'You'd only need two pulleys if you could fix a pendulum to the lamp post in between. It's out of line, but it wouldn't matter if you hung weights or something to take up the slack . . .'

Ruby, now twelve years old and still sucking her thumb, was brainier than ever. Ruby, small, red-headed and quiet, owned a hammer and a Swiss army knife, loved books and maps and numbers and patterns and words from other languages. She was good at mending things too. Ruby knew how to fix charms on bracelets, chains on bicycles, and frozen computer screens with petrified mice. She was an only child, both her parents were dead, killed in an accident when she was a very small baby. Then an amazing and unusual thing had happened. Her four grandparents (all retired, all elderly, all astonishingly intelligent) had pooled their not-very-large

3

savings and bought a house. And into it they had moved with Ruby. All four of them. So Ruby was brought up with not much money but with lots of books, nursery rhymes in five different languages, kitchen chemistry, seaside expeditions to observe the effect of the moon on the tides, and a large floppy cat, bought in order to stop her feeling too much of an only child. Really though, it was her friends who did that. They shared with her and teased her, and at school they stopped her ever having to do a thing by herself. That was very useful to Ruby, because as well as being brainier than ever, she was also shyer than ever.

Perfectly happy though, until the day of her last school report.

Just like all her friends, Ruby had ripped open the brown envelope and unfolded her report the moment she left the school gates.

The first time she read it (eyes round with disbelief), she thought, *how amazing!*

The second time, with Caddy reading over her shoulder, she thought, *but awful!*

She became aware that her heart was beating very fast.

'Ruby!' Caddy had exclaimed, when she finally understood the report's staggering conclusion. 'Do you think you'll do it?'

Ruby did not answer at once. The pounding in her heart was now so loud it seemed strange that Caddy did not hear it too. Her astonished mind was still tottering between AMAZING and AWFUL.

'It would change things a lot if you did,' said Caddy, and then noticed the frightened look on Ruby's face.

'Don't worry!' she exclaimed. 'We'd still be friends! Just as much . . . in a way.'

Ruby stared at her, eyes wide and shocked.

'You'd be posh!' said Caddy, and laughed a little, to encourage Ruby to laugh too.

'Posh!' repeated Ruby.

'I was only joking. Anyway, you already are, a bit. Well, you've got a posh cat! So, will you do it? Would you like it?'

By now, Ruby's heart was bumping less fiercely. Her mind had stopped its tottering between AMAZING and AWFUL. It came down firmly on the side of AWFUL.

'No I wouldn't like it!' she said. 'And I won't do it!'

'Don't you even . . .'

'And I don't want to talk about it, either! So there!'

'I don't see why . . .'

'Please, Caddy,' begged Ruby.

'All right,' said Caddy.

*

5

Beth is perfect.

'I'm not,' protested Beth, neat-haired, brown-skinned, modest as well as perfect. 'I'm not . . . If I told you some of the things I think . . .' Her voice trailed away. She never would tell. She was ungrudgingly nice, even to her little sister Juliet (who preferred the name Jools and was far from perfect).

Beth's parents were also perfect. Her mother was good at homework and cakes for school fairs, and her father always won the fathers' race on sports day. To complete this perfection, and best of all, there was a pony named Treacle, a perfect birthday surprise that had appeared when Beth was eight.

'Of course, he's to share,' Beth was told at the time. 'When Juliet's old enough.'

Juliet was nine now, and Beth would have shared, but, 'No thanks very much!' said Juliet.

Last of the friends came Caddy. Cadmium Gold Casson. Caddy had no special label. She wasn't perfect or clever and she didn't hate anyone. For a long time she was just Caddy, which bothered her friends.

'Just Caddy is fine,' protested Caddy. 'It's what I am.'

All the same, they found her a label, mostly because of her fearlessness with spiders. Caddy was sorry for spiders,

6

so universally unloved, and she didn't allow them to be squashed.

'Leave them to me,' she would command, and no matter how grey-legged, scrabbling, or hairy, she would gently pick the monsters up and carry them to a place of safety.

'Caddy, the bravest of the brave,' said Alison, Ruby and Beth.

'I'm just Caddy really,' said Caddy, but she liked having a label all the same. She felt it gave her a proper place in the circle of friends.

'Alison, Ruby, Beth and me,' she would say to her little sister and brother, Saffron and Indigo, and told them stories about Treacle the pony, Wizard, Ruby's enormous cat, and the tank of miniature fish they could sometimes glimpse through Alison's bedroom window: tiny rose and blue flickering things, like swift-trailing flames.

'I call them The Undead,' said Alison.

'*Oh, Alison!*'

'Well, they do die.'

'Then what do you do?'

'Scoop 'em out, and put some more in,' said Alison. 'Don't look like that! It's life.'

Alison was a fatalist. She could live with the possibility of almost anything. For nearly four years, ever since she was

7

eight, she had lived with a For Sale board outside her house and never shown the slightest interest in its existence. So completely did she manage to ignore it that after the first shock of its arrival, her friends ignored it too.

Years passed. The board faded, acquired a greenish tinge, and became part of the landscape. Then in its fourth year it blew down. A bright new replacement appeared in its place and Alison's friends woke up like a startled flock of birds.

'You're not really moving, Alison? Alison! Why?'

Alison shrugged.

'You wouldn't go far away?'

'Maybe. I don't know.'

'Haven't you *asked*?'

'Asked who?'

'Your parents, of course! They must have said something! Haven't they told you anything, Alison?'

'They go on and on,' said Alison, yawning.

'On and on about *where*?'

'South.'

'South?'

'Where my uncle lives. It's got a weird name.'

To be continued . . .